DEDICATION

For Louie, my late husband. A Prince among men. *"I shall love you, forever and a day."*

I'd also like to thank Whiskey Creek Press, my personal editor and wonderful mother, Fontaine Wallace, David & Greg, Dawn & Ben, Mel & Dick and the entire Campanelli, Wallace family. To God be the glory!

"If you have faith as small as a mustard seed, nothing will be impossible for you."

Matthew 17:19-21

CHAPTER 1

As he glanced down at his left side, Prince Louis watched the blood trickle where his heavy armor failed to protect him.

The horse buckled beneath him, breathing heavily, slowly dying. Prince Louis pulled himself from his raven stallion and falteringly tried to stand. Before him, in the distance, loomed the tall keep of Valtearea; his heart leaped at the sight of the castle just beyond his reach.

His eyes scanned the gatehouse towers as two mounted knights rushed toward him.

"Perhaps I shall live long enough to arrive home."

"My Prince!" the two soldiers cried out, galloping nearby.

"I'll alert King Delaney," one of the knights announced as he turned his steed.

The other knight reached down a hand. "Allow me to carry you!" *The castle isn't far now.*

"No, I shall walk to greet my brother," Louis responded.

Slowly they trudged their way to the castle grounds with the concerned warrior supporting his wounded prince.

Through the large wooden doors bolted a man in royal blue, his surcoat fluttering, the small band of crown tilting on his head.

"Louis!" he screamed at the sight, rushing to embrace him.

"Call for his wife, Princess Bella!" King Delaney ordered the nearest attendant.

Louis could hear the whispers among those in the courtyard. He did not raise his head to see the grimaces at the sight of his weakened condition. Suddenly, a cry pierced the air—Bella.

What has happened to me? I was once known as the fiercest man alive, but Crusader life is proving far more deadly than being wicked, Prince Louis surmised ironically.

"No!" the familiar voice screamed as the castle's huge keep doors banged open. Her gray eyes told Louis all he needed to know. He glanced over her rosy cheeks, her long raven hair and luscious feminine figure. Oh, what curves his wife hid beneath the folds of that green dress! If only he could see them clearly, again. "Good morning, my wife." He gasped. "It seems I have lost our battle."

"It cannot be." Princess Bella sobbed as she watched the guard lift her husband and carry him up the stairs to their royal bedchamber. Louis was carefully laid upon the tiger-skin sheets. Bella's trembling hands held one of his as strong male attendants secured his limbs.

From the corner of his eye, Louis noticed the apothecary assistant approach with a fiery red rod to cauterize the deep wound. A small block of wood was inserted in his mouth, and Louis clenched his teeth upon it. At the intense pain of the hot iron, the prince let out an agonizing cry and lurched involuntarily. He bit into the wooden block, trying desperately not to pass out from the pain.

Finally, he composed himself, willing his mind to ignore the agony. He looked up at Bella whose face betrayed the terror she felt. Louis forced a smile to calm her. "Try not to be saddened if my days of battle and glory be over, my good wife."

Bella's lips turned upward. "If you do not live, then I shall be upset, my Lord. I care nothing for the Crusader battles as much as you."

Suddenly the light began to fade before his eyes; he struggled to focus on her face, which was disappearing into the darkness. "I love you," he softly whispered. For the first time, Louis knew fear.

"And I, you." She gently kissed his dirt-covered cheek.

Again, pain seared his side as the assistant began to check the flesh around the cauterized wound.

So, this is what dying is like? Thunder roared from behind the door. *Thunder, but there is no rain, is there?*

King Delaney rushed to the window. "Who dares come to bring down my brother?" Panic resounded in his voice.

"Horses, my King?" Princess Bella asked.

"The Heathens have followed. They march at our gate! I must prepare our knights. Pull Louis' bed into the hidden chamber behind the tapestry," Delaney ordered a few knights. "Protect him and the princess there. We must remain as keepers of the Shroud."

Prince Louis had heard enough. In between short gasps he spoke, "Brother, you cannot reason with these men. Have a knight offer them gold instead of the Shroud. They may retreat not knowing the Shroud's true worth. They are too skilled in battle... escape by the river... and take my wife with you."

"I must defend our castle!" King Delaney of Valtearea announced with a quavering voice.

Louis felt his bed rising and then being shoved into an opening behind the wall. A woven tapestry of flowers and fruit draped down over the hidden opening. Left in the small room, he overheard the screams and cries from outside.

The prince glanced around. "Wife, are you here? Bella?" Trying to sit up, Louis managed to roll out of bed, hitting his head on the wood with a mighty thump. Darkness engulfed him as he lay motionless on the hard, cold floor.

CHAPTER 2

Louis woke to find his body surrounded by flames. He could barely see through the smoke. The light from the spreading fire was blinding him. Coughing and clutching at the pain from his side wound, Louis crawled to where he thought the door was. He tried to push it open but couldn't.

Quickly, he peered through a crack in the wood and found that a wooden beam had fallen against the door. He was trapped inside the hidden hallway. He stood, covering his mouth and nose, trying not to breathe in the thick smoke.

At the end of the hall, the flames were consuming the walls. He would not be able to get through it. He neared the window, stuck out his head and gulped in some clean air. He looked down and thought it too high to jump.

His eyes trailed down to the courtyard where before him lay knight after knight, bloody and dead. Delaney in royal blue was on top of the pile of corpses. Prince Louis sank back into the smoky hall. The King of Valtearea was dead. His brother dead! *And what of my wife, Princess Bella?*

Louis cried out, the pain searing through him, mixed with rage.

Suddenly a shadow moved past him. He felt a chilling draft in the hot air. Through the smoke came a dark hand with golden gauntlets.

"Take my hand," a deep voice said.

"Brodan?" the prince asked.

"It is I," the shadow answered. "The shroud has been taken."

Louis didn't care about the shroud at the moment, only the death of his brother and whereabouts of his wife. He remembered when Delaney and he were merely children practicing combat. Delaney would never hurt him. He was too kind a boy that grew up to become only too naïve a king.

Dark arms suddenly surrounded him. Fire neared Louis's feet. Faster than flames, the shadowy figure lifted Louis and carried him to the window. They jumped out.

Louis saw the sky as they fell, the spiffs of white clouds mixed with smoke floating above. The sun was bright and large, shining down onto the castle which was burning to the ground. There was a loud smack against the earth from Brodan's feet. Louis's eyes turned to the cloaked dark face; black eyes were staring back at him.

"Remember who you are," Brodan said, lowering Louis to stand on the ground. "The protector."

Louis stepped away and began searching for his wife's body over the blood-stained grass. "Bella!"

"We must go retrieve the shroud!" Brodan reminded.

At this moment, Jesus' burial shroud was the last thing on his mind. His only thought was finding his wife, alive. There were horse tracks, hundreds of them, leading away from the gatehouse. He could follow them and discover if his wife still lived.

Brodan grabbed his shoulder. Louis tried to yank it off, until he saw what Brodan was pointing to with his other hand. On the ground was a piece of fabric, green like the dress Bella had last worn while mending his wound.

His wound? He checked his side. The wound had stopped bleeding. He would live all right, long enough to seek revenge for those who'd set his castle on fire and murdered the Valtearean people.

"Your heart grows cold," Brodan said, releasing the grip on his shoulder.

"Leave me be. I never wish to see thee again!"

Brodan's eyes tightened. "But we must find the shroud."

"Your God let this happen. He destroyed my brother, my land, my castle, my people and now he has let these Heathens, who only want to sell that shroud, take my wife! I do not want to be the protector of the shroud anymore. Do you understand me?" Tears came to his eyes. "Tell your God to pick someone else."

"You don't know what you are saying." Brodan lowered his eyes. "You were chosen."

Louis turned and climbed up the pile of dead men, rushing to the one lying on top. He pushed away the arms of other men and rolled the king, his brother, over. King Delaney's eyes flickered opened. Delaney grabbed his bleeding head and sat up. His attention turned to the castle, falling to the ground in ash and in fiery sheets.

"Our home."

Prince Louis noticed more blood pouring from the head wound.

"It appears our men died protecting your kingdom."

"Where is the shroud?" King Delaney asked.

"Taken."

King Delaney stood, looking around in horror at the death surrounding him.

Prince Louis rose, turned and saw that Brodan had vanished.

"Then we must go after it! Take back what belongs to the Christian people," Delaney said. "That shroud is a reminder of what Jesus did on the cross for them."

"My wife," Louis informed, "has vanished."

"Good." Delaney sighed.

"Good?" Louis was livid. "How can you say that Brother?"

"That means Princess Bella is not dead. Now I know you will follow them and help me get back the shroud."

CHAPTER 3

Louis hurried to the stables. Through burning walls, he saw a mule pulling at his ropes which were tied to the floor. Louis rushed in and untied the animal. Quickly, he grabbed the nearest saddle, tossed it over the mule's back and jumped on. With a kick from Louis' boots, the mule ran out of the fiery stable and past Delaney.

"Where are you going, Brother?" King Delaney asked. "You go without me? Is that how it is? Let me remind you that I am still king! What you own is mine! Bring me that mule! It is mine."

"King of what, firey ash?" Louis lifted his hand toward the crumbling keep. "I take it you'll be fine since the flames didn't scorch your pompousness."

"Get down from that mule! I'm going to Cambone. Our sister's husband will help us gather who's left of our Crusaders. I will go there. Ask him to build us a larger army of knights."

"Go, King! Run to sister's new husband and our mother Queen Fontaine. King Cambone's knights will fail against these Heathens!"

"And what better plan have you?" Delaney wanted to know.

"None," Louis admitted. "But I shall not waste my days kissing ass to King Cambone for help. My wife is in the hands of ungodly men. She might be being tortured as we speak."

"It is more important we bring assistance to take back what belongs to the Christian people."

Prince Louis kicked his mule in the direction of the horse tracks, following them over the grass and sand.

"I demand you stop, Louis!" King Delaney yelled. "Brother!"

Prince Louis rode away at a mule's pace. Traveling from Valtearea, he could still see the horse tracks. He did not give much thought to all those who had lost their lives today. He was too worried about Princess Bella. Delaney may be right. Perhaps it was better to bring a larger army. What could one man do? But he could not risk leaving his wife in the hands of such men a moment longer.

He had heard the heathens were a motley crew. They went from nation to nation, stealing horses, gold and anything sellable for their plight. They were nothing more than pirates on land, Vikings without conscience. And he would be against them, alone, with a mule.

Suddenly, his beast stopped.

Louis kicked its side, and the mule didn't inch forward. Louis dismounted and looked into the beast's face. Its gray fur was covered with ash. It was breathing heavily.

"All right, rest for now…Good for Nothing Mule. I guess I don't have a choice in the matter."

Louis lowered himself to the horse tracks, leaning over them. He realized they split into two directions. Most of the horses went in one direction; only a few went north. North was a tavern. Ah, yes, a tavern, what better way to mingle with the enemy? Royals celebrate with ale.

He looked at his clothes, bloodied and dark. On the back of the mule's blackened saddle there was a leather bag. He tossed it open. Inside were the clothes of a blacksmith with an apron. Perfect.

Quickly, he undressed. As he was raising his arms to remove his shirt, his side began twitching. Louis gazed down to what remained of his side wound where his wife had cleansed it. If it hadn't been for her and Brodan, surely, he would have died earlier in the day.

Slowly, he redressed in a black-scooped shirt, a pair of plain colored pants, and mounted the mule. He kicked its sides and pulled the reins for the mule to go north. The mule headed in the opposite direction, following the tracks of the greater company.

"You good for nothing, excuse for a horse! Go where I tell you!" He tugged the reins to go north.

The mule grunted but continued east.

After several kicks and tugs at the reins, Louis finally jumped off the mule. The mule grunted again and stopped, tucking his head in argument.

"Mule!" The big gray animal made a strange hee-haw sound.

"Fine, then I walk." Louis went north, trailing after the fewer tracks toward a tavern he knew of. There, he hoped to gain information about where they were taking Princess Bella, and the name of the man who took her.

He glanced back; the mule was following him.

CHAPTER 4

Prince Louis walked until he came to a stream. He bent over the water and noticed how different he appeared in the blacksmith's attire. From out of his boot, he pulled a knife and began to shave off his bushy black goatee and mustache. He hadn't been without facial hair since he was a boy. He hoped no one would recognize his clean-cut face.

Louis gazed at his reflection in the stream. His face had changed over the years—more wrinkles, but his eyes were still hazel and his short hair the same dark brown. He gripped the knife and began shaving his head. Handfuls of hair fell to the ground at his feet until Louis was completely bald.

Slowly, Louis ran his fingertips over his hairless head and face as he peered down at his reflection. Now, not even his knights could recognize him. Louis appeared not as a prince but a blacksmith: a younger man who shaves his head to escape the spark of the blacksmith's fire. The only thing a few might recognize was the color of his eyes.

He bent over the apron, took the knife and cut off a two-inch chunk. Then he cut a strip of leather for a strap. Poking a hole in the larger piece, he pulled the strap through and created an eye patch. Louis affixed it above his right eye, and it came down to cover the top half of his cheek.

The change was unbelievable. Louis did not recognize the man staring back at him. He bent over and drank from the stream and noticed the mule drinking next to him. The beast appeared dirty, more so than he had been just miles before.

Prince Louis grabbed some dirt and rubbed it across his face and neck.

The rougher he looked, too, the better.

He rose, grabbed the reins and began pulling the mule further downstream. They went on for several minutes until they reached the forest. The horse tracks were lost among the leaves. Still, Louis knew where they were headed—the tavern with expensive ale and cheap wenches.

It wasn't long before they arrived at the small wooden tavern with a few horses tied up on front posts. On their saddles was the sign of the Heathen—a two-headed snake encircling a long, silver sword.

Louis tied his mule up to a post between the snake-decorated horses.

The tavern door swung open and a large man with a round belly stumbled out. He wasn't in chainmail but in plain clothes that smelled of ale.

"Evening," he greeted as he went to the Heathen horse next to Louis' mule.

Was it evening? Louis hadn't even noticed the sun setting.

"You a blacksmith from Valtearea?" the man asked.

Knowing most blacksmiths were traveling men for hire, Louis immediately answered without fear. "Aye, I am."

"Lost your job then." The man moved his arms around his big belly to untie his horse. "Not much work for a dead king."

The stranger mounted his horse. Before heading off, he said, "King Lightenwood drinks in the tavern. He needs work done in the land of Jacksvilla. He'll pay you in gold coins to remove welded up statues and build swords with our own symbol."

They've taken the castle Jacksvilla as their own? Louis' heart sank with the news. It wasn't only Valtearea destroyed; now Jacksvilla, another large nation, was under their control. Delaney must warn his sister's husband before the Heathens tried for Cambone. Surely, that kingdom could be next.

"Well?" he asked. "For enough, I will work for him," Louis agreed.

"Tell him Coal sent you."

"All right, and how will I know this king?" Louis yelled after the man.

"Look for the man with the golden snake wrapped around his neck." Coal chuckled.

Prince Louis watched him ride off. His disguise surely had fooled Coal; perhaps it was good enough to fool this, King Lightenwood. *King, indeed,he is nothing but a Heathen, a blood thirsty killer who may know where Bella is.*

Louis pushed his mule out of the way and walked up to the door. A patron leaving opened it and he slipped in among the many men. None of them were in chainmail or wearing the two-headed snake symbol. How would he know his enemy?

The prince took in a deep calming breath. Those who looked at him simply glanced away. It was working. His one eye scanned the bar and found a man at the end; he was tall, muscular, with short brown hair and blue eyes. He looked familiar, although Prince Louis couldn't place where he had seen the man before. Around his neck curled a large yellow snake with reddish eyes.

Louis walked fearlessly to the self-made king and said, "Coal sent me to you."

"And how do you know my loyal servant?" The man raised his blue eyes and stared at Louis' dirty face.

"He said you have work for a blacksmith, removal of welded statues in a place called Jacksvilla. I want pay, four gold coins a day, and I'll do it, do it fast." Prince Louis disguised his voice, trying to lower it in case he had ever spoken to him as prince.

The snake turned toward him and hissed. Louis didn't move. He stared into the yellow python's red eyes until the snake curled back around Lightenwood's neck.

"My name is Lightenwood. Would you have a problem calling me king?"

"King? No, no, Sir, not for four gold coins a day."

King Lightenwood chuckled then turned to the muscular, longhaired knight sitting beside him. "Take him to Jacksvilla; show him what to do. Give him what he wants."

The man stood. "Aye, come…what is your name?"

Louis couldn't believe the size of the man. His head equaled this stranger's forearm. "Bellino."

"Like Princess Bella." King Lightenwood chuckled. "You'll do, Bellino. I even like your name: a reminder of whom I stole from Prince Louis Vincent. But if your blacksmith work is unsatisfactory, you'll be pulling those gold coins out of your ass."

"Don't worry, my king, I won't disappoint you." With that, Prince Louis walked towards the door with the long-haired, blond man. He quickly looked back over his shoulder, to the enemy's face he wished he could place.

Had he seen this man, this King Lightenwood before?

Regardless, Lightenwood was the one who had taken his wife. That's all he needed to know. The Heathens were taking over Jacksvilla as their own nation. Princess Bella might be there. That's where he would save her and then murder this self-proclaimed king.

CHAPTER 5

"All you've got is that little mule?" the blond knight asked.

"She takes me where I need to go." Louis glanced up while untying his beast.

The soldier unhooked a white stallion with a long flowing mane and the double-headed snake emblem on its leather saddle.

"Ugly donkey." He sighed.

Louis growled. "What's your name?"

"My name is William. Sir William Lawry, First Knight to King Lightenwood. And what is yours?"

Louis thought of his wife's name and vengeance spelled backwards. "Bellino Ecnaegnev."

"Odd name for a Blacksmith. From what province are you from?" Sir Lawry began to ride away.

Prince Louis kicked his mule, but the beast didn't move. He tried again, but the mule let out a grunt and took only one step.

The white horse stopped, and the blond knight looked over his shoulder. "This is going to be a long journey. Do all your ugly females give you such a hard time?" The prince rolled his eyes, wishing to stab William Lawry through the heart.

Sir Lawry unsheathed his sword and placed the tip on the belly of the mule, inches from Louis' leg.

"Follow me or die, Mule."

Louis stared at the blade. It was thinner than his bulky sword, with ridges on the end. He'd never seen a sword like this. No wonder all his men had died. One strike of a sword like this and when they pulled it back, it would make a gashing hole instead of a clean cut. The soldier who had struck his side did not have a sword like this, or he would be dead.

"You've never seen a blade like this, have you?" Sir Lawry asked.

"Nay."

"It's one of three our king designed for us. Do you think you could make this?"

Never, Louis thought. "Aye, simple."

Sir Lawry pulled back the sword and showed him the handle. Within the steel was what looked like a grip, with indents for fingers.

"This gives us a better grip."

Louis nodded. "Looks light as a feather, too."

Instead of letting Louis hold it, Lawry sheathed his sword and nudged his horse forward. This time when Louis kicked the mule, it followed. Louis wondered why. Perhaps even something as stupid as a mule could figure out that William Lawry was dangerous.

"You are from Valtearea, right?" the knight asked without looking at him. "That was the only castle left in this province."

"I was."

"Did you see the great battle against Prince Louis Vincent?"

"Some of it," he lied. "I left once I heard King Delaney was dead."

"By now, that castle is nothing more than ashes. King Delaney and Prince Louis, the Be header are dust."

Prince Louis' mouth curled into a smile. There was a time, he thought, he would have thought this man a good opponent. But not today, not when he needed time to find his wife and know that she was safe. "Valtearea is dead then. Good riddance. They pay badly. A silver coin is all I got per week."

Sir Lawry chuckled. "The royals are all in ashy graves but the prince's wife."

"A good woman, I've been told. Is your king planning to dispose of her, too?" Louis held his breath as his heart pounded with the question.

"Princess Bella and her maid were discovered carrying some sort of burial cloth from a dead Jewish carpenter. Can you imagine that?" he bellowed, and then calmed his cackling. "Our king stopped her and demanded all of her husband's property now that Prince Louis is gone. She refused. She said where the shroud goes, so does she. She would protect it with her life."

Horrified, Prince Louis gulped. That sounded like her; Bella never knew when to shut up even to save her own life. Louis immediately asked, "So she's going to be killed then?"

"Nay, our king took a liking to her. He said a woman so strong needed taming. He murdered her maid, ordered us to tie the princess up, and then boasted how he has everything of Louis Vincent's after all."

"So Lightenwood has something against Prince Louis Vincent?"

As the horse and mule began heading down the dirt path through the trees, Sir Lawry answered, saying, "Whatever it is, it's enough to make him sell his wife as a whore to the highest bidder."

"A fate worse than death." Prince Louis gulped.

Sir Lawry smiled. "Our troops split tonight. The others go to Landing castle to prepare dinner for King Lightenwood. Soon we shall all meet back in Jacksvilla to try and prepare to overthrow King Cambone. Then King Lightenwood shall own every kingdom. We shall become stronger than Rome, Egypt or Camelot. Be thankful, Bellino. With us, there will be much work with good pay. Perhaps you can even afford more than that ass between your legs."

Louis wondered which one he was referring too. "Aye, I've come to the right place."

CHAPTER 6

It didn't take long for Louis to grow tired of riding the boney mule; he was exhausted and so was the beast. Gingerly, Louis dismounted and began pulling the mule after Sir Lawry and his reliable steed.

The pair continued until they reached Jacksvilla. Louis stared at the upcoming castle, and it made him sick. He remembered Jacksvilla as it was with signs of the cross hanging in every window. What was left of the keep now? A burnt building, a curtained wall, and a massive colorful two-headed snake pennon hanging in front.

"Isn't this castle beautiful, Bellino?" Sir Lawry asked. "The Keep has four floors."

"Indeed."

The knight pressed forward to the wooden doors of the curtained wall. Immediately, the gate opened for Sir Lawry. Servants rushed towards him and snatched his reins. Sir Lawry dismounted and turned, waiting for Louis. When Louis reached the gate, a servant came forward to assist with the mule. Prince Louis gladly handed her over. He didn't get two steps before he heard the servant cussing because the mule would not go any further.

Sir Lawry laughed and then put his hand on Louis' shoulder.

"Come, let me show you Jacksvilla."

Louis trailed after him; his eyes locked on every knight walking the wall above, making sure no enemies recognized him. There must have been dozens of men, every few hundred feet. No army could travel close to the castle without these soldiers spotting them from miles away.

"Some of the crusaders' quarters were burnt, but we're rebuilding. For now, the servants are sleeping on the bottom floor of our keep," Sir Lawry said as they walked into the tall square building.

Louis looked into several rooms. They were small and had two cots against each stone wall. When he passed the third room, Lawry stopped.

"This will be your residence while you work," Lawry said. Louis looked the room over. Two cots, no window, stone walls and wooden floor and that was it. Not even a chair. He would have never put anyone in such a small cold space.

Sir Lawry took the stairs. Louis followed to the second floor. There they passed a kitchen, a storage room, and finally came to a grand hall of dining. Sir Lawry moved into the giant room and opened his arms.

Louis had never seen such a beautiful dining hall before. There were glass windows with pictures on them of Jesus and the Saints. Iron statues high on the walls, held up by steel rods that went all the way to the ceiling. Even the fireplace was made of stone, the mantle iron held an imprint of the last supper. This must have been Jacksvilla's chapel, Louis realized.

"I'm sure you can see why Lightenwood needs your services to remove all this. This is all for the King of the Jews and not for our king."

"Aye." Louis thought the art which a tribute to Christ was breath-takingly beautiful.

"Our king wants you to rebuild the mantle and replace the figures with that of a two-headed golden snake and likenesses of him. Are you able?"

Louis couldn't recall the last time he held a hammer. "Of course."

"Good." Sir Lawry led him back to the storage room which contained piles of metal and wooden chairs. "Your tools are somewhere in this mess. You'll have to look for them. Be quick about it. King Lightenwood and the others come soon. They'll want to see you working to change the hall into something more suitable."

"I see."

"Before you begin, let me show you the third floor." Sir Lawry motioned him to follow. Together, they went up the stairs. "You will never be allowed farther than this, but I want you to meet your roommate."

"What of the fourth floor?" Prince Louis asked.

"That is the dungeon."

The third floor was the royal chambers with guards in front, and across the hall was a throne room; a throne sat in the middle made of twisting golden snakes. Someone in the corner was painting on the floor. What had already been brushed disgusted Louis. There were pictures of King Lightenwood in battle, killing men, burning castles and images of dying naked women.

Sir Lawry walked over to the young man crouched on the floor. Beside him were bowls of flowers and roots smashed to make colors. In his hand was a brush that smelled of horse mane.

"Christopher, this is Bellino, our new Blacksmith."

The young man with brown hair didn't look up, but Louis didn't care. What he was painting curled Louis' stomach and made him have to fight not to be sick. The man was painting a likeness of him engulfed in flames.

Next to Louis' image was King Lightenwood with a sword, stabbing him through his side.

"Christopher, I am speaking to you!"

Christopher looked up and Louis recognized him, despite the tears on the young man's face. He hadn't seen him since he was a child, thirteen perhaps. Christopher had been his sister's ward until he vanished into the night, upset over some argument. Clearly, he was still alive. His sister would praise the very sight of him.

His eyes had changed a bit; they had dark circles around them as if he had been through hell.

"Christopher, this is the man you will be sharing your room with— Bellino."

Christopher wiped his eyes to better see him. Chains rattled at his feet as he rose to his feet. "Christopher Vincent Cambone, I am. Son of a King." Slowly, his eyes moved to Louis'.

"What's the matter with Christopher this fine day?" Sir Lawry said, hardly seeming to care that the young man was near tears. "You don't like painting your dead uncle? You're lucky we took you back before we murdered a lot of the Christians." He nodded, reluctantly, and then lowered himself to continue painting.

Christopher hadn't recognized him. Louis hardly would have known him either; how thin and pale, a young man he'd become. Being a slave to Heathens and painting their victories had taken its toll.

Sir Lawry reached out and yanked up the boy's plain brown shirt over his back. Below were flagrum marks, fresh, bloody and scabbed. "You see, this is what happens to you if you try to run. We'll chain and reprimand you. This one ran to warn Prince Louis Vincent of our troops coming from the north. Foolish boy, wasn't he?"

Christopher's tears streamed down into the face of Prince Louis being painted below.

"Now he works for crumbs of bread instead of someday wearing the Cambone crown." Sir Lawry shoved Christopher back down.

Louis' rage boiled beneath his skin, crawling down his spine in one painful wave. Sir Lawry would face his blade, he concluded, because of the torturous acts he had committed against his nephew.

Chapter 7

Louis dismissed himself from Sir Lawry. "If you don't mind, Sir, I'd like to work now."

Christopher raised his head for a moment. Louis wondered if Christopher recognized his voice. Then Christopher's chin lowered, and he continued painting on the floor.

Prince Louis walked away without looking back. He never wanted to enter this room again. To see the blood and destruction painted made his stomach churn. He hurried down to the storage room and went through some barrels. In one of them was a large axe.

He entered the Grand Hall and enjoyed the beauty of it again. Even Valtearea didn't have such an amazing chapel. Suddenly, he heard trumpets blaring from outside. He rushed to the stained-glass window, and through a pane of pale blue, he glimpsed several large wooden carriages and knights arriving on horseback.

Someone tapped him on the shoulder. He turned to discover Sir Lawry was behind him. "I told the cook to prepare your meals with the rest of the servants. Servants are fed after the knights. You'll be paid each night with your meal." Sir Lawry gazed through the window.

"Thank you, Sir."

"Now go. The king comes early."

Prince Louis wanted to see if Bella was in the entourage.

"Shouldn't I start right away?"

Just then, the doors to the castle swung open, admitting dozens of knights. They went to the tables and began banging on them.

Servants began rushing from adjoining doors with baskets of wine and bread in their hands. Then, he entered, the dark-haired man with the giant golden snake wrapped around his neck. Servants bowed to King Lightenwood as he approached the head table at the end of the hall. Knights stood and lowered their heads silently.

"My Lord." Sir Lawry bowed. "What a pleasant surprise to see you in Jacksvilla."

"This is a time to celebrate with my men. We shall drink and eat in glory of the destruction of Valtearea!" King Lightenwood declared.

The knights cheered as King Lightenwood strolled further across the dining hall and sat at the front table.

Prince Louis suddenly got the urge to run and strike Lightenwood's head with the ax, but then he heard a scuffle of small feet and pivoted to the door again.

Slowly approaching was the woman who touched his heart like no other. Princess Bella was covered in soot. Her green dress was ripped at the hem. His anger left, replaced by the need to protect her.

Bella strolled between the tables of knights. They all watched her every move, and so did Louis. Amazingly, she didn't appear frightened. Her head was held high with her shoulders back.

"Beautiful, isn't she?" Sir Lawry whispered in Louis' ear. Prince Louis didn't answer, for what he saw upset him. She strolled to stand in front of King Lightenwood.

"As princess, I dine with kings," she said. "If it is time for me to eat, I'll need a space at the Royals table."

King Lightenwood frowned. He grabbed a basket of bread from a servant and held it out to Bella. "Feed my men, Wench."

"I am not your slave."

"Oh, yes, you are." King Lightenwood shoved the basket into her arms, nearly knocking her to the ground.

Prince Louis heard the knights laugh.

Bella faced them. "You have no manners on how to treat a princess."

King Lightenwood stood, and all the men stopped laughing. There was rage in his eyes. "How dare you call yourself royalty in my presence?"

"Don't you raise your evil voice at me!" she spat at him.

"Heathen!"

King Lightenwood's mouth opened in shock. He stared at her with disbelief.

Louis tried to hide his anguish for he knew her well. Bella was a woman with a sharp tongue, this he admired. He had almost forgotten how unlike other women she was. Lightenwood, however, wouldn't enjoy her strength.

"Do you have any idea of what I am capable? I could snap my fingers and strike you dead faster than fire bolts in the sky," King Lightenwood reminded.

Bella grabbed her bodice and said, "Strike me through the heart that is broken already. You are a murderer, a thief of love, a destroyer of all that is good and holy."

King Lightenwood's eyes were locked on her bosom. He had to close his eyes to regain control of the argument. "Serve my men or I shall burn that burial shroud and make you into my whore."

Princess Bella grabbed the basket of bread and began throwing bread toward each knight. The noise of goblets falling over and smashing against the table made Louis jump. As she turned toward him, he saw her eyes. The gray eyes were red and fighting back tears.

Prince Louis sighed. No, she was not as strong as she was pretending to be. She was upset and she was hiding it through her rage. Tears fell openly as she walked and tossed bread at Sir Lawry and him.

Finally, a knight grabbed her wrist and forced her to drop the breadbasket before she could throw another loaf. Louis recognized the man who'd told him to see King Lightenwood for a job. He recalled the man's name was Coal.

Princess Bella let go of the bread and spit on his face. Coal quickly drew his sword. Louis leaped forward, holding the ax, but Sir Lawry grabbed his shoulder.

"Coal!" screamed Lawry. "Wipe your face and let her be. She lost her means today. Her spirit's yet broken; you should be so strong."

Coal wiped his face and released her.

"Leave, Princess!" King Lightenwood ordered. "Until you know your place."

Weeping, Bella stumbled towards the open door. She turned and cried out, "It's about time you called me 'Princess,' for I am wife to Prince Louis Vincent of Valtearea, dead or not!" Her legs buckled and she fell into a heap weeping on the floor.

Lightenwood returned to his meal, as did the knights.

CHAPTER 8

Prince Louis cautiously walked toward his wife curled up in a ball on the floor. Sir Lawry yanked him back.

"Are you still loyal to Prince Louis?"

"I'm on my way to my room. You told me to wait to work until morning. Remember?" Louis faced him.

Sir Lawry's blue eyes tightened. "Begin at dawn."

Prince Louis moved closer to Bella. He wished she'd look up. Of all people, she would know him. For a moment he slowed, hoping she'd recognize his plain brown boots. He took another step, listening to her cry. If she'd just raise her head, she'd see him. She'd know he'd never abandon her.

"Don't weep, Love," he would say. "I'm here. I'm all right." Glancing over his shoulder, Sir Lawry scowled at him. The words he wished to speak would never come, Louis realized.

He returned to his room and found Christopher lying on the cot to the right. Louis plopped on the other bed. "What's your name again?" he asked, pretending not to know him.

No response.

"I take it you're upset about what happened with Sir Lawry." Prince Louis wondered if he should tell him who he really was.

"Valtearea was my uncle's home," Christopher softly said. "Is it true about Princess Bella, my aunt? Was she captured? Is she here?"

Prince Louis said, "Aye. I just saw her in the dining hall."

Christopher added, "Then I must find a way to help her escape. King Lightenwood will only harm her. She is a good woman, a faithful one to my uncle."

"Don't be foolish, boy."

"I'm not a boy," Christopher said with a snarl. "And you don't understand. She's family. I'm Princess Sharera's son or at least I used to be." Christopher propped up on an elbow.

Louis remembered when Christopher was a boy, he would play with a small sword in the courtyard of Valtearea. Christopher would be brave, fighting enemies, protecting Valteara against evil men. He had been a good ward to his sister, until the day he ran away.

"Sir Lawry will kill you."

"I have no other family but her now," Christopher said.

Louis smiled. "Princess Sharera married. Since her husband Cambone's become king, she lives in his castle, not Valtearea. Your mother lives as does Queen Fontaine."

"My mother told me she would stay in Valtearea after she wed."

"Perhaps her new husband persuaded her."

"My mother thinks me dead, or she'd have sent my Uncle Prince Louis Vincent after me." Christopher shook his head. "I have no chance now. I have no life more to give."

"You're a painter," Louis praised. "I've never seen such detail before. You should be proud of that and want to live for your art."

"What do I draw but blood and death, victories of the Heathens? They aren't masterpieces. Better to risk what breath I have to save my aunt, Princess Bella."

"How'd you come to be in this state, boy?" Prince Louis asked.

"I lusted over a farmer's daughter. She was beautiful. She had very large…" his hands cupped over his breasts, "and a sweet smile, which curved more on one side. The last night I met her by the cornfield, Heathens on horseback were blazing her home, claiming it was theirs to burn. My girl ran up to the riders yelling something. I couldn't make out what through the horses' ruckus. I tried to grab her. A Heathen snatched me from behind and put me in chains."

"What happened to the girl you once loved?" Louis asked.

Christopher grimaced. "They slit her throat. That is why I must save my aunt. This King Lightenwood could do the same to her."

Louis took in a deep breath; the thought of his wife's throat severed outraged him. "They'll have to get through hell fire first."

Christopher was staring at Louis' disgusted frown. His eyes were locked onto his jaw, his one eye and dirty nose. "The way you speak, you remind me of someone." His eyes continued down his face.

Prince Louis rolled slowly on his bed to face the wall. He noticed then it was made of thick hay and not very comfortable.

"Bellino?" Christopher asked.

"Aye."

"Has anyone ever told you, you look a little like my uncle. It's been some time since I've seen Prince Louis Vincent, but there is a resemblance." Christopher sat up, trying to catch another glimpse of Louis' face.

Prince Louis laughed. "Me? Boy, you jest."

"Like Prince Louis Vincent."

"When was the last time you saw Prince Louis, boy?" Louis asked. "The last I did was in Valtearea not long ago; the prince's hair has gone long and gray. His belly is big like King Arthur's."

Christopher leaned over him. "You are right. My memory may not be so good. It's just you do remind me of him."

"Get to bed, boy. We've got work in the morning."

"I am not a boy, but nineteen years." Christopher returned under his blanket. Louis rolled over and found Christopher's eyes closing.

CHAPTER 9

Thoughts of Christopher's warning shook him to the core. Bella could be killed. Prince Louis got up from his bed, went out and peeked into the dining hall. The torches along the wall were lit. A knight was drinking ale at the far end of a dining table. He hurried to the right, glancing in each doorway for Bella. Sleeping men were in their rooms.

Footsteps came behind him. A knight? His hand quickly went to the knife in his boot and whirled around.

"Just wondering where you were going?" Christopher gasped.

"Where are the prisoners kept?" Louis growled.

Christopher slowly backed away.

Louis tucked his knife back in his shoe. "Tell me."

"Will you harm them?"

"Show me where they are!"

"No! You want to hurt them."

"I just want to make sure your aunt is all right," Louis said. "After what you told me, I fear she may be in danger."

"You worry as I?" Christopher asked. "She'd be kept in the tower, which is the dungeon for the aristocrats or enemies of the King. This hole has one prison in the tower's fourth floor for the rich and one deep in the bowels of the keep for the most dangerous of criminals who are left without nourishment to die."

"Will you help me?"

Christopher started upstairs. Louis followed, watching closely for knights behind. At the second floor, there were two men with long swords sleeping in the stairwell. They reeked of ale.

One snored a loud grunt. Christopher stopped. Louis placed a hand on Christopher's shoulder and motioned him to move onward.

On the fourth floor, Christopher pointed to the last room and whispered, "That's where they would keep any woman of value."

"Get back to your room. Keep quiet." Louis tiptoed down the hall and into the chamber.

Even in the darkness it didn't take him long to find her. She was sitting near a windowsill, in a giant cage made of iron. Her face was dirty, and her dress was torn. Still, she was every bit as beautiful as the first day they'd met. Her dark hair, long and black, curled to the waist and shined like a raven's feathers in the moonlight. Her small facial features and her long neck took his breath away, even now.

With her straight posture and chin raised, to the world she might appear oblivious to her situation. But Louis noticed, ever so slightly, that she was biting her lower lip. He knew she was fighting back tears. The wood creaked below his foot. Bella turned and gasped.

"Who goes there?"

"Are you alright?" Louis disguised his voice. "Has anyone hurt you?" Louis reached out and examined the lock. It was as big as his hand and so thick, even an ax wouldn't break it. He'd needed the key.

"Lightenwood has harmed me."

The hair on the back of Louis' head stood up. He slowly released the lock and asked, "How so?"

"He's murdered my husband and stolen the burial shroud. You have no idea how important they are to me and my people." Bella came forward.

Prince Louis immediately stuck his hand into the cage to try to touch her. "I know."

"Your hands smell of ash," she said.

"I've become Lightenwood's blacksmith since Valtearea's fall." Louis wished his hand could find her.

She moved her soft fingers over his hand, clasping it. "My fellow Valtearean. Then we are in this together, you and I."

"Aye."

"Do me this, take the shroud from this devil who's stolen it." Louis wished she hadn't said that.

"I beg of thee!" One thing became clear to him. She wouldn't leave Jacksvilla until she had dragged the bloody cloth with her.

"You should be worried about yourself, not a dead man's linen."

"If you'd come from Valtearea you'd know what that cloth is and what it reminds us of—that Jesus Christ died for us. You'd try to save it! You'd do it without question," Bella said.

He let out a long sigh, released her hand and turned to leave. "I am from your kingdom, my Princess. But you are in a cage. I can't in good conscience leave you in this predicament for long."

Louis went into the hall, his heart heavy laden.

CHAPTER 10

A rooster's crowing woke Prince Louis. He sat up to find Christopher staring at him. He checked his eye patch. It was secure. Quickly, he went tothe door and peered down the hall. Sir Lawry was standing at a table.

"Bellino," Christopher said. "Can I ask you something?" Louis ignored his nephew and hurried to the knight.

"I told you to be here at dawn," Sir Lawry's voice snipped. "The cock has crowed."

"My apologies, sir," Louis said. "I must be tired from my journey."

"While you slept, I took the liberty of getting your tools." Sir Lawry pointed to a table. "King Lightenwood had a word with me. From now on, he wants you to work through meals from dawn 'til dusk. You will get only short breaks. Do you understand?"

"Aye." Louis grimaced.

"Take down the stained-glass windows by any means necessary. They are most repulsive to our king."

Louis moved around Lawry and examined the table. An ax, a hammer, a fire iron and a mallet, anything he'd need to destroy the intricate glass windows. He gripped the ax, wondering if this should be a tool, he'll use to kill Sir Lawry, run upstairs, and strike the lock to free his wife. Grabbing the ax, he whirled around. No one was in the hall; the knight had gone.

He wandered to the window. Different fragments of colored glass formed a picture of Saint Francis. A red cardinal bird was in his hand and a white rabbit sat at his feet.

"Louis," called a familiar voice.

He glanced over his shoulder and found another Lightenwood knight, with the golden two-headed snake embroidered above his chainmail. But the face was not of a stranger; it was that of a dark-skinned hairless man with ebony eyes.

"Brodan? Have you become a betrayer to all that is good?"

"I will never betray Christ. I'm here in disguise, as you are, my Prince." Brodan moved closer. "Will that be so easy to do for you? Can you destroy the picture window of our beloved Saint Francis?"

Prince Louis raised the ax and struck the window as hard as he could. Instantly panes shattered, falling to the ground and breaking into millions of shards. The noise was deafening. He leaned out of the empty window and gazed upon the picture of Francis reduced to a mess outside on the grass.

"That was much too easy for you," Brodan said, disappointedly.

"Leave me alone! I protected that shroud with my life and how does God repay me? He burns down my kingdom and allows the wicked to keep my wife in a dungeon!"

"He feels your suffering. He is with you always."

"These Heathens are murderers. Jesus can't save them, that linen, or me." Prince Louis went to the next glass window of Mother Mary, standing with her arms outstretched. She was wearing a white and blue robe, her hair hidden beneath her headdress.

"He will save you. Why do you humans only see what you want and not that there's a larger purpose?" Brodan inquired.

Prince Louis slammed the ax against the glass. The window fell his way this time, covering him and the floor. He felt cuts across his arms, his shoulders and his head. Angrily, he turned to face Brodan. Brodan hadn't a scratch on him.

"I no longer want to understand," Louis said. He went to the next window. This time, he didn't even look to see what the picture was of. He lifted the ax. Instantly, it was pushed back and dropped behind him to the cement floor. He glanced up and saw that Brodan was standing in front of a glass picture of Jesus' crucifixion. Somehow, he had pushed the ax back.

Louis recaptured it and threw the ax over Brodan's shoulder. It broke Jesus' arm and flew into the grass. Slowly, pane-by-pane, the picture of Jesus dropped.

Brodan grabbed Louis and whirled him around to see the face of Jesus crashing to the stone floor.

"Bellino!" In his ear cried a man's voice.

Louis turned to discover Brodan wasn't holding his shoulders, but Sir Lawry was.

"Are you alright?" the knight asked. "You're covered in blood."

Louis checked his face. He pulled back his hand to find his fingers dripping red.

His blood was shed for you. The prince heard Brodan's voice like a whisper and then it was gone.

"It's no wonder why you lost an eye. You've got no sense in that head of yours." Sir Lawry plucked a small piece of glass out of Louis' cheek. He sighed. "Perhaps being blind would be a significant option with a face that ugly."

Prince Louis suddenly wished the ax were still in his hands.

"Clean up all this mess, including your face, before our king arrives for his breakfast."

"Aye, Sir," Louis lowered his bleeding head in compliance.

CHAPTER 11

As Louis swept the floor clear of the colored glass shards, King Lightenwood entered the Grand Hall with the golden snake encircling his neck. He sauntered to the head table underneath the shattered window and he sat down. Almost immediately, a servant rushed forward and handed him a small, live quail with a broken wing.

The king grabbed the giant gold snake and placed it next to the quail. At once, the creature opened its mouth, unhooking its jaws. Long fangs snapped onto the bird and the snake proceeded to swallow the doomed animal whole.

Louis tried not to stare as he bent over to sweep the glass into a pan, but the snake's actions proved quite intriguing. The last gulp, the bent wing, slowly descended the snake's long yellow length.

As soon as the king raised his hand, the servant returned with another bird on a golden plate; this cooked one the king pulled apart with his fingers and ate with satisfaction.

Searching for his wife, Louis began observing the serving wenches; it didn't take him long to spot the torn dress that she had been wearing yesterday. Though her hair was uncombed, her face had been washed. A serving helper handed Bella a basket of apples and pushed her towards the tables. *Trouble.* The knights hadn't learned from the last time she had been given bread to serve.

"Staring at her again, are we?" Sir Lawry observed from nearby. He always seemed aware of what Louis was doing.

Prince Louis had been so busy watching his wife that he had forgotten to continue sweeping. "Sorry, my Lord, I will finish my work."

Sir Lawry walked to the nearest table and sat down. A wench quickly put down a plate and served him a succulent quail. He gave quick thanks under his breath and then waved Bella closer, saying, "An apple, Wench!"

Bella walked over; as she did so, she raised a small red fruit to her lips. She took a bite of it then slammed it down on his plate beside the bird; she then proceeded to the next knight, took a bite of his apple, and almost tossed it down to the table. She repeated this at each setting as juice dripped down her chin. What amazed Louis was that the knights weren't angered; they accepted the already-bitten apples as edible fare.

When she went to the head table where King Lightenwood was last to be served, she searched the basket. On his plate, she left a brownish withered fruit, one with a long, gray worm crawling out.

"Full?" King Lightenwood pinched her posterior and cupped one buttock.

Anger raged through Louis. He brushed the last of the glass fragments into the pan, unable to watch the exchange between them.

"Bellino!" the king called Louis.

Louis approached King Lightenwood's seat, wishing he could punch him in his face. How he would love to see the look on the king's face as he showed the disrespect the leader rightly deserved. "Yes, My Lord," he answered obsequiously instead.

"The sun coming through is hot with the glass gone. Find something to cover the window."

Where can I find a drape so long? Louis wondered.

At that moment, Sir Lawry stood and addressed Louis. "Fetch me the brown linen bag from my room, last door on the left. That should suffice."

Louis dropped the pan and scampered down the hall. He was biting his lip, outraged and warming quickly. Bella wasn't a servant; she was a princess, and a royal more powerful than Lightenwood ever would be. How dare he lay a hand on her!

Prince Louis opened the door to the last room in the hall, one twice as large as his. It housed a large bed, two windows and a table for writing. There on the bed lay a rather large brown leather pouch. He picked it up and plodded back to the grand hall where he handed the bundle to Sir Lawry. Sir Lawry untied the bag and pulled out a long, blood-stained linen. Louis recognized it at once.

"Hang this so our king will suffer discomfort no longer," Sir Lawry said, handing the cloth over.

After collecting the shroud, Prince Louis approached the empty table nearest the gaping window opening and then quickly stepped onto the top. He bent down, grabbed the shroud along with his hammer and nails. He raised the cloth over the window and began nailing the outside edge to the frame. Soon the cloth covered the window, shading the morning light as the rays crept across the floor. The glowing face of Jesus was inches from Louis' eyes.

Suddenly Bella screeched below. "Not the holy shroud! Not that! It isn't a drape!"

Louis heard a bench squeak as he whirled around. King Lightenwood was on his feet. He was laughing. Good, Louis thought, he'd be easier to kill.

Quickly, he jumped off the table and began nailing the bottom of the cloth to the frame of the window.

"With this tasteless decoration we see how strong the King of the Jews truly is," King Lightenwood snarled as he curled the snake around his neck and rose. "Too bad we weren't the ones to kill him," he added spitefully, plodding toward the door.

Bella tossed her apple basket at him. "Monster!" The flung basket hit the king in the chest and spilled fruit in every direction. At once, all the knights rose to their feet, grabbing their swords.

"You have gone too far!" the king roared. "I've been tolerant because I wanted to whore you, myself, and sell you to my brother. You are not worthy!"

Prince Louis gripped the handle on the ax. Whatever Bella's sentence, he'd protect her even if it meant he'd die in the process. He kept his eyes locked on the king, as the sun shining through the shroud rose at his back.

"That fruit will be the last meal you will ever partake in," King Lightenwood announced. At that moment the sunlight moved from the king's chest to the bottom of the snake. Suddenly the reptile hissed loudly. Without visible provocation, the royal snake attacked the king, sinking its giant fangs into the king's cheek.

The king screamed. Immediately, Sir Lawry rushed to his side, ripping off the snake in one quick gesture. It rolled into a ball on the floor and then loosely uncoiled, turning instantly to fiery ash by the sunlight reflecting through the shroud.

Grabbing at his puncture wounds, the king collapsed into Sir Lawry's grasp. Lawry swept him up in his muscular arms and headed down the hall.

All that now remained of the huge reptile was a small pile of grayish ash. The shroud had done this, Louis surmised, but would anyone guess it was Jesus' image, or would they blame his wife? It was she who had tossed the fruit basket that seemed to spook the snake.

CHAPTER 12

It didn't take long for the knights to exit the hall following their king. Louis swept up the snake's ashes, watching the servants eat the knights' leftover food. Bella wasn't eating, however. She stood, staring up at the shroud. Her shimmering eyes focused on it as if she were mesmerized by the relic.

A young servant girl walked over to her and asked Bella, inquisitively, "Was it that cloth that caused the snake to bite the king?"

"It was."

The young girl's eyes grew wider. "Is it magic?"

Bella placed her hand gently on the girl's head and stroked. "It is the love of Jesus Christ that has the power against evil."

"Jesus Christ?" The girl quickly snatched her basket and hurried away without waiting for a final response.

Bella approached King Lightenwood's chair, seated herself and started to dine on the remnants of the king's pheasant. This was a sign of the utmost disrespect, for only the king should dine at the king's table. She gave Louis a scornful look, daring him to stare at her. Then her head bowed to eat the delectable bird left on the plate.

Prince Louis checked to make sure no one else was watching her, but the hall had been cleared. Everyone but the servants had gone upstairs to make sure that the king would live through the snake's bitter deep bite. Louis swept closer to the table, wanting desperately to tell her who he was and that he was going to save her.

Princess Bella ripped off another piece of meat and began devouring it. "Would you like some?" she asked him. "Is that why you keep staring at me? Are you hungry?"

Louis shook his head. In a deepened, disguised voice, he said, "Not for food."

"Eat if you like. Servant's food isn't half this good." Bella took another bite of the king's bread. "In Valtearea, we treated all our people with dignity, and everyone received the same food."

Louis deepened his voice further to disguise his tone.

"I remember."

She put down the bread loaf. "Was it you who visited me last night? I was told you are the blacksmith from Valtearea." She touched his arm, studying his muscles then his face covered with an eye patch and scruffy beard. Tears suddenly came into her eyes.

"You have strong arms like my dead husband." She sat back deep in reflection.

"Are you sure Prince Louis is dead?"

"I saw the castle burning myself. He was inside. I tried to run upstairs to save him, but the soldiers restrained me." She pointed to the linen hanging in the window. "Did you see what its power did to that wicked king and his snake?"

Louis nodded and faced her. But she wasn't paying him much attention anymore, only to the cloth in the window. How he wanted her to! *Just look at me, Wife*, he wanted to say. *Can't you see me underneath this disguise? I'm alive, just look at me.*

"You don't remind me of any blacksmith from Valtearea that I recall." Bella's eyes tightened down onto her dinner. "You're hairier than Jacob and far more larger than Eli. Which blacksmith master did you work under?"

"Bellino!"

The sharp snapping sound of Sir Lawry's voice grated on his very last nerve. Slowly, Prince Louis turned on a heel to find the knight standing behind him. Sir Lawry's shirt was still bloodied from the king's face wound. "I was cleaning up the ashes, Sir. How else can I be of service?"

"Forget the dead snake," Sir Lawry said scornfully. "Take that drape down from the window."

Louis noticed Lawry staying to the side and out of the light from the shrouded window. He wondered if Lawry guessed that the sun through the burial cloth had caused the snake to bite the wicked king.

"Come, Bella. I'll take you back to your dungeon. You will be punished for eating the king's food!" Sir Lawry demanded, still standing back.

She pulled the plate closer to her and started to eat again, ignoring the command completely. "What did you say? My ears must have failed me."

Louis realized that Bella must be aware of Lawry's fear of the shroud, too.

"Come here! Don't make me come to you!" Lawry demanded, stomping his very large boot on the wooden floor.

"I'll leave the king's table when I feel like it."

"Bella!"

"Frustrating isn't she," Prince Louis whispered to him, knowing just how far she could drive a man mad. He chuckled beneath his breath. Bella gave him a nasty look and then continued dining on the king's quail. Fearlessly, she slowly chewed, enjoying every bite at her leisure.

"Bring her to me," Sir Lawry ordered him.

Louis pondered for a moment, knowing he had to follow orders. With a mighty swing he grabbed her arm, forced her to rise and pushed her toward Sir Lawry.

"You, insolent bastard, don't you have any devotion to your princess?" Bella grimaced. "Visit me no more."

Sir Lawry stopped. "This man came to you? When?"

Princess Bella turned and looked down. After a long silence, she lied, "Just now, didn't you see him talking to me? I never want to eat with him again!"

Why had she just protected him? Louis wondered.

"Take down that cloth, Bellino. Burn it. Bury it. Just get rid of it! I don't want it in this castle again—ever!" Sir Lawry shouted. "I'll be back after I teach this woman a grave lesson!"

"Do what you will to me, but don't harm the shroud!" Bella reared back, trying to pull her arm out of Louis' grasp.

"You want to die, Woman?" Sir Lawry asked, infected by her recklessness.

"Oh, let me have her!" Louis begged with more enthusiasm than judgment. "I haven't had a woman in such a long time!"

"Having someone as you would be worse than a flag ram whipping." She pouted. A slow grin grew on Sir Lawry's face.

"I'll ride her harder than a mule," Louis promised, wanting to have a moment with Bella to tell her who he was and why he was there.

She screamed, raised her hand and slapped Louis square in the jaw. "You wouldn't dare! You disgusting Pig!"

Sir Lawry laughed, amused. "All right, Bellino. After you get rid of the cloth in the window, you can have the night to take a whore. I don't have the time to deal with this now. The king is ill and has lost a lot of blood. He needs me now."

"You wouldn't!" Bella roared.

"Yes, Sir." Louis then snorted like a pig. "It will be my pleasure."

CHAPTER 13

Louis could sense Sir Lawry's belittling stare observing him like a hawk as soon as he returned to the dining hall. It must not have taken the knight long to return Bella to her prison cell, Louis thought.

Pulling the second nail out of the shroud, Louis' hands moved to catch the linen before it fell from the window. But the cloth didn't move. Without even a nail, the cloth still clung in the window.

"Pull it down!" Sir Lawry barked, with a scornful look.

Prince Louis jumped down from the table, yanking the shroud with him; he rolled it into his arms like a long drape. With more enthusiasm than judgment, Louis confided his discovery: "The shroud is warm."

Sir Lawry's hand reached out, but quickly pulled back before his fingers touched its warmth. "Get rid of that damnable thing," he barked.

Louis gracefully retreated to the front door; he could hear Sir Lawry's feet crunching behind him. It would have been so easy to outrun such a large fellow. No, he would try escaping for only the one thing that mattered: his wife.

"Put it in this," Sir Lawry ordered.

Louis pivoted and found that the knight was holding out his wife's brown leather bag. He wasn't sure if he should contain the long linen because Sir Lawry might not be afraid of it covered. Slowly, Louis grabbed the bag, flipped open the leather cover, and stuffed the cloth in, not caring if it wrinkled.

"Good." Sir Lawry reached for the bag. "We shall—" The knight never finished his sentence; he dropped the bag, and in a flash of fear stepped back.

"Sir? Is something amiss?"

"Its heat can still be felt," Sir Lawry said, his jaw literally dropping.

"It was well heated by the sun," Louis responded. "I shall take care of it for you. I will bury it, Sir. That way if the king finds a buyer for it, I can dig it up and bring it to the buyer myself. Would that please King Lightenwood?"

Sir Lawry nodded; his face crinkled as he pondered. "That is what he wanted it for, to sell. The Crusaders will pay a king's ransom once they discover their Christian relic and Valtearea have been ravaged."

"That is what I shall do then." Louis walked out into the grounds. He went to the first tall tree in front of the castle. Its leaves were round, and the trunk was covered in a twisted heart-shaped, leafy vine. Louis decided on this tree because the unusual vine made it different from the other trees. He would easily be able to retrieve the shroud again. Louis stopped before the imposing tree, turned and walked three paces to the right. He dropped to the long grass and began digging a hole about twelve inches in diameter.

Sir Lawry remained in the doorway, not coming closer, as if he were frightened. "I had heard that the linen was different," he muttered.

Louis pretended not to know of the rumors surrounding the cloth. "Really, what have you heard regarding this?"

"That if you believe in Jesus that nothing is impossible to you. The shroud can heal the sick and cure the weary-hearted." Louis was surprised Sir Lawry was aware of its rumored power. His gaze tightened and he stole a furtive glance at the knight.

"Perhaps it is faith that does that."

"You think me a fool for repeating such gossip," the knight responded grimly.

"Nay." Louis regarded him with sympathetic eyes.

"I know what I saw," Sir Lawry said. "The king's snake is not poisonous, yet the king's face swells with boils. I cannot explain why this cloth feels alive either. Its warmth is too strong to be from the sun. You know it as well as I, do you not?" Louis did not respond, but he continued digging. The dirt was hard and needed his full attention in order to be skillfully dug.

"What power does this bloody linen have? The Valtearean people were more worried about it than their own king. I stabbed King Delaney myself. Instead of fighting back, Delaney tossed the cloth to Princess Bella and instructed her to run. When I chased her down, Bella screamed something about leaving the shroud for her people. Why does she care for it that much to be willing to give her life for it?"

"You question like a believer," the prince commented.

"I am a follower of King Lightenwood. I will do as he demands, worship whom he wants. Still, I must admit that over all my years, I've seen heads of kings mounted on pikes and worshiped, I've seen every animal, Merlin's tricks, even stones held sacred. None are like this relic," Sir Lawry admitted. "Do not breathe a word of what I say."

Louis took the bag and dropped it in the appropriately sized hole. Trying not to be obvious, he refastened the top to make sure no dirt would touch the linen. Then he began pushing the soil and grass back over the bag until it was completely buried.

"You come from Valtearea, Bellino. You must know someone who can teach me of this cloth's powers."

Louis rose to his feet, pivoted around, and grumbled, "Garments of death have caused me nothing but grief." Sir Lawry approached Louis and gripped his shoulders.

"How so with this one?"

Louis urgently protested. "Remove your hands from me, my Lord. I will speak no more of this."

"You dare give an order?" Sir Lawry slapped Louis' face. Feeling the sting, Louis walked around him, ignoring the strike.

"I am anxious to have that woman," he announced.

"I think not," the knight responded icily.

Suddenly, Louis felt a cold blade rising over his shoulder to his neck. Forced to stop or have his throat sliced, he countered, "Sir, you did give your word." Sir Lawry pulled a set of keys from off his belt, dangling them in front of Louis' eyes.

"I'll need those," Louis concluded.

"Not anymore."

"You said I could have the princess after I buried the shroud!"

"I have changed my mind. She will be my teacher now."

"Teacher?" Louis grimaced.

"Yes, the princess will instruct me of its powers. Tell me more of this Jesus."

Louis realized he could not go to her, unlock her cage, and sneak her out. Sir Lawry's change of heart was ruining their chance of escape. "We made an agreement," he challenged.

Sir Lawry sheathed his sword, hitched up the keys and pulled out a palm full of gold coins. "I am a man of my word. I only promised you a whore. She is not one. This will buy you ten at the tavern. Go, I give you the night."

Louis stood there with the gold pieces in his hand. It was enough to rebuild a castle and Lawry gave it to him as if it was a pittance. Louis watched Lawry return into the fortress remembering how he himself once held such passion for Christianity. At least, now, with Sir Lawry interested in what his wife had to say, she should be safe from his sword.

Louis' stomach churned, however, as he remembered Bella's temper. No, he thought, they were not out of danger yet. Bella might not be cooperative.

CHAPTER 14

Sir Lawry returned to the castle, leaving Louis standing over the now-buried shroud. Louis bent down, picked up a large white rock, and placed it over where the cloth was hidden. The stone would be its marker.

Sitting above on a thick tree branch and adorned in a brown cloak, Brodan suddenly appeared. The vines wrapped around his legs as he sighed and said, "For someone who doesn't care, you are going to great lengths to be able to find Jesus' shroud again."

"Go away," Prince Louis retorted belligerently.

After a long silence, Brodan replied flatly, "I am an angel sent to watch over the shroud. I left it for Simon Peter and the other followers in the tomb, true believers, not for a person whose heart grows blacker each day."

"Have I suffered no less than Simon Peter?" Louis recalled how he had lost everything, his home, his title and even his wife to King Lightenwood. Not wanting to hear another word, Louis stormed toward the stables and entered there. Among the tall, svelte horses was the boney donkey that had brought him. He grunted at the beast of burden and carried on. He needed to find a fast horse to be able to escape with his wife. Searching through the stable, he remembered Raven, his stallion that had died in the fierce battle. Once considered the fastest horse in all the land, Raven had survived many wars in his short life.

Among Lightenwood's horses he found Sir Lawry's white mare. The horse was big, but brawny. His head was long for its neck, but its big brown eyes had no fire. "You won't do," Louis muttered to the animal.

Beside that white horse, another stallion stood. It had a long black mane, thin sturdy legs and a well-proportioned frame. Louis gave it a noncommittal smile. "What about you?"

"That one's mine." A short man with long black hair, a fat nose and missing a front tooth stumbled into the stable torch light. In one hand, he clutched a goblet of ale and in the other, a big red apple.

Quickly, Louis patted the horse appreciatively, feeling the thick muscles below the neck. He gazed into its face, and they infected each other with recklessness. "A fine specimen this one is."

"What is it you're doing here?" The man raised an apple to his lips, grunted, and waited for an answer while gazing at Louis.

"He's the Blacksmith from Valtearea," interrupted a stable boy, mucking out a nearby stall.

"Just checking on my donkey when I came across this one," Louis announced, calmly and feigning disinterest.

"My name's Mick," the stable boy said. "And he's Bellino."

"I'm Sir Henry." The older man took another bite. "That's my brother's son."

Louis guessed the boy's age to be about nine. Mick had short red hair and lots of freckles. The shirt he wore was brown which closely matched the hay stains across the front. "How did you know who I am?"

"I know everything," Mick said. "I hear everything."

"Shouldn't you be working inside?" Sir Henry asked Louis. "We already have a blacksmith that takes care of the king's horses."

"I was given the night off," Prince Louis announced, flatly, after a brief pause. "I thought I would go to the tavern."

"Aye, for the whores. Good ones there. Ask for Sassy the Lassy." His mouth bulged with fruit as he spoke and chewed at the same time. Juice ran down Sir Henry's chin and he nonchalantly wiped it with the back of his hand.

"So how did you get such a fine mare? Did the king give it as a gift?" Louis asked, wondering how the man could afford such a fine animal.

"I am the king's messenger, Sir Henry Demont. I ride like the wind on this fine steed."

"Aye, a messenger's horse." That made sense. Of course, a deliverer would have the finest, fastest animal in Lightenwood's castle.

"Only the swiftest you've ever seen," Sir Henry gloated, gulping down some ale after his last bite. "I've beaten even the kings in races."

This brown beauty with the black mane would become his, Louis decided. He took one last glance, remembering the horse stall was the last, three down from his old donkey. "What's its name?"

"Excaliber."

"Like King Arthur's sword." Louis recalled the stories of the king from Camelot.

"Let's hope Bellino lasts longer than that Blacksmith Walter." Mick suddenly chuckled.

Sir Henry laughed at the Stable Boy's comment and then pivoted back to Louis. "There isn't a castle on this earth King Lightenwood hasn't stolen from or destroyed. He plans to kill the royalty in Cambone next. Then, King Lightenwood shall rule over all the lands."

Lightenwood plans to murder my sister? My Sharera! Louis' heart began to pound with the dreadful news. Sweat beaded on his brow, and then he slowly questioned, "Why those in Cambone?"

"Haven't you heard? Queen Sharera claims to be a Christian. She's a fool," Sir Henry muttered with distaste.

If this had been a different place and time, this man's head would have already splattered onto the hay. Louis feigned nonchalance and asked, "When is this to take place, this great new adventure to Cambone?"

"I'll be the one sending word to the knights. It will be soon enough. Would you like to ride along?"

"Perhaps," Louis lied, hoping there would be no war at all. Then he turned to face the short man who was biting on the vestigial core of the apple.

"You better find something better to ride than that sad excuse for an animal if you come with me," Sir Henry added while chewing.

"Indeed." Louis nodded in agreement. He retreated gracefully and then climbed up the small hill covered with lilies which was next to the castle. He sat down at the crest, watching day turn to night. From this height, it was easy to spy Bella's chamber; two shadows were flickering in candlelight. Was Sir Lawry still conversing with her? Louis wondered. What would happen now that his sister's castle was next on King Lightenwood's destroy list? There wasn't much time left to save Bella and help lead his sister's army against this wicked king.

His brother, King Delaney, had been right. They did need the help from Cambone's army to defeat King Lightenwood.

He lay down on the grass and stared up at the stars.

Soon, dreams came... his sister's emerald, green eyes fluttering in fear; her red hair being hooded while hands tightened a rope around her thin neck. To the loud crash of the boards dropping, he sprang awake. A bee was buzzing over his head. Quickly, he swatted the pest away, looking down toward the castle.

The sun was rising; the night had gone. Below, the courtyard was bustling with knights going about their morning rituals. His old donkey stood near one of them, eating grass.

What a horrible dream!

If his brother Delaney didn't warn Sharera, she would surely be killed! Prince Louis realized that he must rescue Bella and warn his sister himself, before Lightenwood's knights could gather to attack Cambone.

Prince Louis checked to make sure his eye patch was secure. Then, he returned through the heavily scented lilies to the castle's entrance.

He knew that Sir Lawry and the other knights probably thought he'd spent the night in the tavern with cheap women. However, he would never do that—not when he lived and breathed for Princess Bella.

Inside, the knights all seemed very subdued. He noticed them ignoring the wenches and wine set on their dining tables. The king's illness truly was affecting his people.

Prince Louis' uncovered eye skipped among the women. Bella wasn't serving breakfast. He climbed the stairs in search of his wife and Sir Lawry.

When he got to the top, a knight in full armor stopped him with the jab of a hand into his chest. "Where are you going in such a hurry?"

"I need to find Sir Lawry to inquire what my duties are this morning," Louis quickly explained, lowering his head obediently.

"The First Knight sits with the prisoner, the beautiful one from Valtearea," the knight sad and pointed upstairs.

Louis hurried up the steps, down the dark hall and peered inside. Bella was in the dungeon cage, but not alone. She was locked in Sir Lawry's arms, her face against his chest, right above his heart. Lawry was gazing down at her, brushing her hair ever so gently with his fingers.

It was all Louis could do not to burst into the dungeon and yank them apart. Shocked, he gasped, trying to interrupt their embrace.

"Sir, what is my next order?"

Sir Lawry kissed Bella's cheek and then shot him a nasty look.

"Leave us alone!"

Louis tightened his hands into fists. He shuffled across the floor. Biting his lip, he asked with eagerness in his voice, "But, Sir, my duties?"

The knight finally withdrew from Bella's side and then locked the cage after his exit. He approached Prince Louis with a look of scorn.

Bella grabbed the bars, interrupting. "I am looking forward to seeing you again, Jacob."

Jacob? She knows Sir Lawry's first name! Louis felt his face burn with rage as the knight raised a hand and placed it on his shoulder.

"Never bother me again when I'm with Bella." Sir Lawry's voice was a snarl. "I'm sure you're tired from the whores. Take advantage of my good mood and rest until noon, then start removing the statues from the entrance hall."

Louis tried desperately to forget how Sir Lawry had his hands on his wife. Even worse, how she had allowed him. Oh, how he wished to murder the man right now. He'd rip that smirk right off his face—take that hand off his shoulder by slicing it clear off.

"Yes, my Lord." Louis bowed and pivoted to leave, straining to hold his temper while clenching his fists.

CHAPTER 15

In the entrance hall, Louis labored all afternoon trying to knock down an iron statue of the disciple Thomas. It stood a foot off the ground but was welded to the wall with long metal brackets. Removing it was proving no small task.

Deciding to take a break, Louis plopped to the floor, still grasping the ax in his tiring hand. Twelve statues behind a long table with Jesus sitting in the middle decorated a long wall which portrayed The Last Supper. Each statue was fashioned of bent iron and attached with brackets so thick they were nearly impossible to break even with an ax. He had worked half the day and only managed to break one clasp. Now Thomas was merely drooping away from the other statues.

Suddenly, Sir Coal approached, holding a long metal tool in his hand; Louis hadn't seen him since the first night in that tavern. "Try this, Bellino," Coal volunteered as he held it out. "Another blacksmith named Walter fashioned it before King Lightenwood had him beheaded."

Louis carefully examined what Coal had handed him. The metal rod was about two feet in length with a square hole in its circular tip. "What is it?"

"It supposedly removes spikes. I don't know if it will accomplish the task, but you may try."

Louis wondered if he should inquire why the last blacksmith met his demise but decided against further questioning.

"The king has been asking about you, Bellino." Coal scowled.

"He has?" Louis grimaced, wondering if his true identity had already been discovered.

"Yes, he asked me who took down the shroud and I reported that you had performed the feat. He wanted to know if we thought it was the cloth that caused the snake to bite him."

After a long silence, Louis responded flatly, "The serpent did not like the sunlight; that is all."

Coal handed him the giant wrench and pivoted halfway to face the statues. He stared at the statue of Jesus for a moment. With a noncommittal smile, he admitted, "Our king is different now."

"How so?"

"Half his body is full of boils and his skin is turning so dry it resembles the scales of a snake. His head, an arm, and a leg are so revolting I can barely look at him," Coal added in hushed tones.

Returning to the statue of Thomas, Louis put the metal contraption around the last metal spike and turned with all his might. It began lifting out. He repeated the motion until the spike released and Thomas' feet hit the ground with a loud crash. "This tool works!" Louis exclaimed.

"Removing the statues will please our king." Coal walked to the entrance door and opened it. "His Majesty has asked for each to be melted down and fashioned into swords to kill Crusaders." He glanced back over his shoulder to the statue of Jesus.

Louis noticed his visage softening and wondered if he had judged it accurately. "You sound disappointed."

"Where did you bury the shroud?" Coal asked quickly, ignoring the comments.

Louis shrugged and lied. "I don't know, out near the field somewhere. Why?"

"Was it under the tree with the heart-shaped, leafy vine wrapped around it?" Coal pointed out of the entrance door. "Was it the middle tree?"

Louis walked over to the window, peering out into the trees; his eyes bulged at what he discovered. Overnight, giant white flowers had bloomed among the tree's leaves. "Not under that tree," Louis fibbed, hoping to hide the truth.

Coal nodded. "Funny how that tree now grows flowers when the others do not."

"Maybe it blooms this time of year." Louis had seen trees like that before, but they never had flowers before. A miracle!

"What about by that rock?" Coal asked.

Louis lowered his gaze and saw the stone he had placed above the shroud. Surrounding it, tall plants with bright yellow petals had emerged.

"Aren't those sunflowers?" Coal inquired. "Those don't even grow in these parts. Do they? I haven't seen those since I was a boy in England." Coal shuffled across the floor and mumbled, "You buried the shroud there. You are not telling me because Sir Lawry told you to bite your tongue."

"Sir Lawry told me nothing. Perhaps you should ask him," Prince Louis suggested.

"I don't need to," he responded quietly.

With a burst of insight, Louis realized the shroud was beginning to touch lives as it had done in Valtearea's castle so many years before.

Nothing could stop it now. The shroud astounds even unbelievers. "Don't be fooled by its tricks," he admonished.

"It's not a mystery when it's right before my eyes," Sir Coal concluded as he turned and walked away.

CHAPTER 16

Dusk had come and gone. Louis felt driven to remove all of the statues before anyone would wake on the morrow. One by one, the figures fell to the ground with the assistance of his new tool.

After Jesus tumbled, Louis began dragging the disciples out of the castle, one by one. This surely would please Lightenwood. It would better keep his disguise until the right moment when he could try to escape with Bella and the shroud.

Suddenly, a scream came from his small bed quarter down the hall. Chills ran down Louis' spine as he realized the terrifying cry might be coming from his nephew. He ran to their sleeping quarters, wrench in hand, to see what was happening.

King Lightenwood was standing over Christopher's bed, grabbing him by the throat. His nephew was turning blue and gurgling.

"You have a grievance, my King?" Louis asked, afraid for Christopher's life. The king continued to choke the boy.

Louis had to stop him, or Christopher would surely die. He reached out and yanked the king's arm away from Christopher's neck. Outraged, the king spun around. Half the king's face was puffy and scaled like a snakes. Louis backed away, horrified at the king's new appearance.

"Even my servants are terrorized at the very sight of me now." King Lightenwood took in a deep breath.

"Whatever Christopher did, please forgive him."

King Lightenwood headed for the door. "He will hang for what he painted on my throne room floor! Sleep well, Boy, for it will be your last sunrise."

Watching King Lightenwood storm out, Louis moved to lean over the bed. Christopher was grasping his throat and coughing.

"Are you alright?"

"For now," he murmured.

"What did you do to anger him?" the prince asked.

"What I must." Christopher laid his head down, finally catching his breath. Suddenly, Sir Lawry came into the room and snatched Christopher by the arm. "Come! You will be locked in the dungeon."

Christopher glanced back to Louis. "If you should see my mother again, tell her that I'm sorry I ran away and that I always loved her. Oh, and…" He stopped only for a moment. "Thank you. You've been like an uncle."

What had his nephew done so badly to be sentenced to death? What did he paint on the throne room floor? Louis stepped from the doorway in time to see Sir Lawry rush Christopher upstairs.

Louis waited until they were out of sight and slowly trailed after. From the shadows, he spied Sir Lawry shoving Christopher into the chamber across from where Princess Bella was being kept in the dungeon.

The stairs were empty now. Louis ran past the second floor to the throne room. He checked both halls, no one. Then a man moved between the golden chairs, the king, holding a goblet of ale.

Louis didn't have time to retreat.

"Come forward, Blacksmith!" the king ordered. Louis bowed obediently and hurried to the king's side.

"I'm sorry to have disturbed you. I wanted to apologize for stopping you from killing Christopher."

The king laughed. "I should strike you dead for coming before me without being summoned."

Louis dropped to his knees. "Forgive me, I only wish to serve and beg your forgiveness."

"You removed all the statues from the entrance hall. You are a hard worker, Bellino, laboring well past sundown. I shall pardon this disobedience once."

His eyes saw what the king was standing over. It was a painting of the shroud hanging in the window. The snake was biting the king and these words were written to the side, "Revenge is Mine, Sayeth the Lord."

"This is what that foolish boy painted!" The king's voice roared.

King Lightenwood appeared so life-like, the shroud brushed to perfect detail in the painting. It had been done to outrage the king. Christopher had painted his own death sentence.

"It's hideous, my King."

"I know you like him, Bellino. But even a young man must pay for his actions. When I was about his age and not yet made a king, I met a boy named Louis Vincent. He was a prince, son of my father's enemy. I didn't know who he was. I saw him skipping rope in dirty clothes, so I thought him another servant boy like me. I invited him into my home for supper. He seemed thankful until we sat down to eat. Then he grabbed a knife from the table and slit my mother's throat. My father started yelling just in time to be stabbed in the chest. I had thought Louis hungry, and had taken pity on him, when he truly was the assassin of his father, King of Valtearea. Before I had time to retreat, that boy came after me and stabbed me here." The king removed his shirt. His flesh had lost its hair and his neck, face and chest were covered in scales. Among the flaking skin was a scar from a dagger. "Never trust anyone. Prince Louis of Valtearea was so good at disguises even as a boy; I hadn't known my enemy at my own table."

"Prince Louis changed," Louis claimed. "After his father's death. They say he found God."

"Aww, yes." King Lightenwood sat down upon his golden throne, staring down at the floor. "After he stole the shroud and found Jesus, they say. Prince Louis Vincent is dead now, but what have you done with his shroud? Did you destroy that cloth for me?"

"It is gone. You shall never lay eyes on it again."

"Rise." King Lightenwood waved for him to stand. Louis stood with lowered head. "You are a fine servant, Bellino. Even though you seek pity, I will not spare the boy. Christopher is not loyal and further still, he is confessing that he is a Christian now by painting this. Do you understand?"

"Yes, my King."

"If there is one un-loyal servant there could be others. I do not know what occurred with my serpent either. Perhaps it was the sun that angered him or the princess' shouting, I do not know. But if this Jesus, Prince Louis' king did this to me, then he is not for me. And if it was Bella's doing, she will be gone soon enough."

"Gone?"

"Bella Vincent will be sold. Prince Louis has many rich enemies. The price for her to become a slave can buy me ten castles. Since Louis is dead, to harm his wife is the next best thing." The king sighed. "I heard once that King Vincent had riches beyond that of any king hidden in his tomb. They say it even contains living gold. Better yet, perhaps the family will pay for her return, and I can kill them, too."

Louis' heart began pounding. He raised his eyes to Lightenwood, only to find him smiling at the thought of hurting his family.

"Be thankful Christopher shall die. You'll have a room to yourself for a while until another painter can be found to cover this mess up."

CHAPTER 17

His head was pounding with the thoughts of his wife being sold to one of his enemies. Perhaps the buyer wouldn't just keep Bella in a cage and make her a servant to humiliate her. No, it could be far worse.

Even from the hallway, leaving the throne room, Louis could hear his nephew's voice. Over his shoulder, he glanced back to the king who was no longer on his throne but staring out his window drinking wine.

Louis slowly walked up the stairs to the prison, trying to move as quitely as he could so as not to alert the king that he wasn't returning to his empty room.

"I tell you, My Lady, the blacksmith is he," Louis heard his nephew say.

"You are mistaken," Bella answered. "I watched the castle burn. My husband didn't get out. No one could have escaped that fire, and he was out cold half-bleeding to death."

"I know my uncle. It is him. I swear it. He must have come to save you."

"Don't say such lies to me," Bella said.

Louis walked into the prison. Both of them went silent for a moment, staring at him in the doorway. His gaze went to his nephew with his head and hands in a block, then to his wife. A part of him didn't even care if she was in love with Lawry, because he loved her more than life.

"Uncle," Christopher called. "Tell her who you are and why you've come to this horrible place. I figured it out long ago."

Louis went to Christopher. He examined his hands and head, then the piece of wood that was wrapped around his neck. There was a latch behind his head with a giant lock that was chaining him to the wall. Louis took his wrench and stuck it in the circular top of the lock. He slowly pulled the wrench open until the top of the lock was open wide enough to allow the latch up.

Christopher pulled out of the block and immediately hugged him. "Thank you, Uncle. It is you, isn't it?"

"Get outside as silently as you can. Hide behind the tree with all the flowers and wait. If your aunt and I do not come shortly, run back to Cambone castle. It's where your mother is."

Christopher released him and rushed from the dungeon.

Prince Louis slowly turned to face his wife. Her hands lifted outstretched to him. "Tell me who you are."

With one quick swoop, Louis took off his eye patch and came into the light. She saw him as clear as day now. Her tear-filled eyes told him as much. He went to her, and through the bars embraced her, kissed her.

She shivered in his arms; how good she felt. He had wanted this for so long and the moment was finally here. Bella knew he was alive and seemed pleased. She appeared almost as happy as when he had seen her holding Lawry.

Suddenly, Prince Louis pushed her away and stuck his wrench into her lock. Hers was bigger than Christopher's but made the same way. He pulled open the wrench with all his might and the lock raised. Bella reached around the bars and removed the latch underneath. Quickly, she swung open the door. The lock made a loud thudding sound as it closed back down.

Bella rushed to Prince Louis and kissed him again. This time, Louis didn't wrap his arms around her. He took her arm and said, "Come, we must leave this place."

"What about the shroud?" she asked.

"I know where it is."

"We must take it with us. We can't leave without it. King Lightenwood wants to sell it."

"Come." Louis tugged at her arm.

She stood still. "I'm not leaving without that shroud, Louis."

"We'll get it. I know where it is. I buried it myself."

"Buried!" Bella said aghast.

Another voice said, "It lies with the worms."

Louis looked up and saw Sir Lawry in the doorway. He stopped and gripped the wrench in his hand. He'd kill Sir Lawry if he had to, to save Bella's life. Perhaps that was best anyway. To kill the man who had charmed his wife.

"Let us go," Bella asked Sir Lawry. "Please, you know they'll kill me if you don't."

"Step out into the light," Sir Lawry ordered Louis. Prince Louis took a step forward but moved the wrench to behind his back, hiding it.

"So, it is you." Sir Lawry took a deep breath. "Her husband, raised from the dead."

"Aye, I've come for my wife."

"And soon as you leave, you'll dig back up the shroud. Perhaps you think you'll steal some horses, take your nephew and be gone for good, never to return to Jacksvilla? Is that your plan?"

"It was," Louis admitted.

"I suppose if I try to stop you, you'll kill me?"

"I shall."

Sir Lawry put his hand on his sword and slowly pulled it out. Louis brought out the wrench, slowly raising it for a fight to the death. Before Louis took a step towards him, Sir Lawry dropped his sword on the ground.

"Go then, Prince Louis of Valtearea."

"What?" Louis' eyes tightened on Sir Lawry's face in surprise.

"Protect the shroud and make sure Bella is kept safe. I'd rather you rescue her, than my king sells her to someone who may do her harm."

Louis knew then. He took Bella by the arm and moved past Sir Lawry. "You do love my wife."

Bella stopped for a moment in front of Lawry, whispered something and then briefly kissed Sir Lawry's cheek. Louis tugged on Bella's arm, pulling her away from the knight. Watching their closeness, Prince Louis felt his heart break.

CHAPTER 18

Louis crept down the stairs with his wife and nephew checking the rear. When they reached the bottom floor, Louis spied two knights in the dining hall, gnawing on turkey legs. One was Sir Coal.

Louis whispered back, "Wait until I say. We'll run out the doors when the coast is clear."

"He's a strange one," one knight said from the dining hall.

"I could swear I've seen that Blacksmith before."

"I saw Bellino once at the tavern." Sir Coal picked up another turkey leg and rip off the meat with his mouth.

Suddenly, in front of Louis appeared a mist forming into the shape of a man. His shiny dark head was reflecting the fire from the stakes in the wall. Louis showed no surprise or fear.

"Out of our way, Brodan."

"If you try to escape this way, you will be caught. There is another path, a secret passage that leads underneath the castle. No one knows of it. They took control of this castle without realizing half the men fled."

Bella smiled to Brodan and said, "Thank you, my Friend."

Louis noticed the knight next to Coal suddenly rising toward the kitchen. He left his sword leaning against the table.

"Get out of my way, Brodan."

"You must not kill. It is not what our Lord wants. He does not want the shroud protected by bloodshed," Brodan explained.

Louis walked through Brodan's misty form and hurried toward the table. Immediately, he snatched the sword. Sir Coal hadn't even noticed him approaching until the weapon was above his head. Coal dropped to the floor as the sword hit the table in a loud thud.

The other knight rushed in from the kitchen, dropping his turkey leg. Prince Louis screamed to Bella and Christopher, "Run!"

The two hurried for the door. Bella grabbed the latch and tried to open it. She screamed, "It's locked!"

Coal unsheathed a knife and rose. Louis didn't hear Bella's scream as more knights rushed in. It didn't take long for the group to be surrounded, swords pointing from every direction.

Sir Coal ordered, "Grab them."

Two moved closer to capture Bella and Christopher. Louis raised his blade to begin fighting them off.

"Don't you dare!" Sir Lawry roared from above, holding his arm. "For your wife and the boy shall surely die."

Prince Louis knew he was right.

"Surrender, Vincent!" Sir Lawry roared. "And they might have a chance to live."

"Where shall we take them," a knight asked, grasping Bella's arm.

"Take the woman and child back to the prison, lock them up. They can't escape again without Prince Louis." The knights gasped at the name.

"Prince Louis Vincent?" Coal gasped.

"Look, it is him. Look at the face!" The knights for a moment spoke to one another in agreement. It didn't take them long to figure out that since he was wearing the blacksmith's clothes, he had been among them all along.

"What shall we do with our king's greatest enemy?" Coal asked Lawry. The prince waited to hear the words, "kill him."

Sir Lawry descended the stairs.

"Lower your blades. Take care of the woman and boy."

Bella and Christopher were forced back up the stairs. Louis kept his eyes on Sir Lawry instead of the dozens of swords directed at his heart.

Sir Lawry snatched Louis' blade. "The king shall decide your fate."

Louis turned to follow Sir Lawry, but now King Lightenwood was on the bottom step, holding a lantern. His scaled face was scowling with rage.

"You!" he said.

Prince Louis felt the rage seething in him, the hatred for his very soul. "Yes, it is I, Prince Louis Vincent of Valtearea."

The king raised his lantern to stare at Louis' face.

"You!"

"The right of confession is mine," Louis said.

"Is that your last dying wish?"

"I have two."

"I shall not let you say another word!" The king shook with rage.

"I beg of thee, my King, hear my confession."

Shocked that he had called him, "my King," King Lightenwood paused on the stairs. "You have no idea of my hatred of you! For if you did, then you'd know anything you ask of me I'd only do the opposite."

"Please, my King, all I ask is that you hear my confession and grant me one dying wish."

"As a prince, he has that right under Royal law," Sir Lawry reminded.

"Damn Royal laws! I am king!" King Lightenwood shouted.

"Take this prisoner to my throne room. I will hear his confessions in hopes for an apology for what he did to my family long ago. Bring me wine and food! If Louis Vincent wants to confess all his sins, this may take all night."

CHAPTER 19

Prince Louis looked over his shoulder at Bella; tears began streaming down her cheeks. Her eyes met his and together they reflected love's bitter dance. Painfully, Louis turned his gaze away from her and addressed the king.

"I have a dying wish, my King."

"Spit it out," King Lightenwood firmly ordered.

"In my pocket, I hold a bag of gold, over twenty pieces which I have earned since coming to your castle. I would like to return the gold in exchange for knowing my wife won't be sold to another. Many despise me even more than you."

"And who should I give Bella to?" The king scoffed.

"Have mercy on her. Bella is more like you than you think. Do you know how she came to be my wife?" Louis asked. "I killed her people and two of my soldiers sliced off her father's head. Bella didn't love me, until I changed, until she knew I was no longer that evil man."

"Bella, step forward," called the king. The Princess was pushed to stand beside her husband.

Louis could smell the strawberry scent of her hair. He could feel her heat and it radiated through him. He remembered the last time he'd kissed those lips. How good she'd felt in his arms.

"Is what Louis Vincent says true?" the king asked her. "Is Louis responsible for the death of your family as he was mine?"

"I'm afraid that he was partly responsible," Bella admitted. "Although, it was not his hand that made my father's head roll."

"But it was his army that killed your father and took over your family's kingdom long ago?"

"I loved my father." Bella nodded. "It is true."

"I've heard enough, step back," King Lightenwood said. Bella inched away from Louis. Her hand briefly touched his. He glanced at her, and in her eyes, he found tears, as she stepped away.

"I will allow you to pay for Bella's freedom. After all, since you still live, she is legally your wife and your property."

"I don't want to belong to another man," Bella cried out.

"My king," Prince Louis continued. "My final request is that Bella be given to Sir Lawry to be taken as a wife."

King Lightenwood's eyes widened in surprise. "You called me king?"

Bella screamed. "No!"

After a moment to compose himself, the king waved to his First Knight. "Sir Lawry, come forward." The knight knelt down in front of King Lightenwood, next to Louis.

"My King."

King Lightenwood was silent for a moment. He drank another gulp of ale. Slowly, he returned the goblet back to the table. "You heard Louis Vincent's final request. I will not force you to marry such a wicked woman unless it is what you wish. Do you want to be responsible for such a woman? Do you want to take on that burden of a wife?"

King Lightenwood clearly meant to talk Sir Lawry out of it, but Sir Lawry answered, "I will take care of Bella as best I can, My King. I humbly accept the offer."

"Will you be good to her?" Louis asked Sir Lawry, turning his head to his once nemesis. Sir Lawry looked directly into Prince Louis' eyes.

"Will you love her? Will you promise never to hurt her and take care of her even when she is sick, to understand her when she is sad, and embrace her when she has need?" Louis continued, his eyes filling with tears.

"I promise you that no harm will ever come to her."

"Good," Louis said. "She is a beauty, but she has spirit. Be prepared for her to anger you. Behind that fire is a woman worthy of great love."

"I know." Sir Lawry raised his hand and put it on Prince Louis' shoulder. "Your last request shall be granted. She will always be loved by family."

King Lightenwood interrupted them. "Then it shall be done. Sir Lawry, take the coins and hand them to me. I will deem that you paid for Bella to be Sir Lawry's wife. It is done. You shall die, Louis Vincent, knowing that Bella will live."

Prince Louis let out a breath, tears streaming down his face. He looked around. The knights still had puzzled looks on their faces. Bella began crying as Sir Lawry pushed his hand into Prince Louis' pocket for the gold.

Sir Lawry pulled out the gold coins and carried them to the king on top of his throne. He left the payment and then went to Bella's side.

Louis noticed that there were tears running down Sir Lawry's cheeks as well. *Tears of joy?*

"When you killed my parents, you didn't care for anything but blood. You may be a changed man, Louis Vincent. Still, you and your nephew Christopher must pay for the crimes which you have committed in my kingdom," King Lightenwood said. "Today at dusk, you and your nephew shall be hung. The shroud shall be burned in front of your eyes."

"You can't!" Bella screamed.

Sir Lawry said, "King, Louis Vincent buried it, and I don't know where the shroud is."

Louis waited until the noise from the onlookers quieted. "Then I ask this, spare the life of my nephew Christopher for the where abouts of where I buried the shroud."

"I'll die for the shroud," Christopher said. "Don't tell him, Uncle!"

From the onlookers, the Stable Boy Mick came forward. "I am one of your stable hands, my King, I watched him bury it. The shroud is under a rock. I know where it is."

"Good. Go, get it," the king ordered. The young man bowed, and Louis shook his head with disappointment.

"As I was saying, both you and Christopher shall be hung as the shroud burns. Your hangman shall be the very woman you spared. Know this, Louis, your wife will be the one to pull the latch that will make you dangle."

"My King? One more thing."

"What?"

"Forgive me for killing your parents," Louis said.

CHAPTER 20

Louis and Christopher were taken to the dungeon. Louis was put inside the wooden block and Christopher was placed in the dungeon cage. Louis sank to sit on his rump and leaned the block of wood against the wall to rest. His hands were already starting to fall asleep from his wrists being locked in the holes.

"Uncle, it's best if you stand and keep moving."

"I'll be fine," Louis said.

Christopher moved to the bars closest to Louis. "Thank you for trying to save my life."

Louis nodded, his mind on Bella becoming another man's wife.

"That was good of you to save my aunt."

Ignoring his nephew, Louis realized the only way out of dying tomorrow was to break free of this block of wood. He began to bang it against the wall in hopes that the wood would break. Wham! He hit the wall hard and his neck took the weight of the hit.

"Don't do that, Uncle!" Christopher said. "You'll break your neck or wrists."

"What difference does it make? All of me will be dead tomorrow if I don't get out of this contraption."

"You'll be dead soon enough breaking your neck."

Prince Louis leaned back against the wall, knowing his nephew was right. He was trapped and there was nothing he could do about it. He looked down at the chains shackling his feet, perhaps there was a weak link. He began moving his legs, trying to see if there were any cracks in the iron rings.

"Do you think they'd put you in chains that you could break," Christopher questioned.

"Silence!" Prince Louis roared in frustration.

"Talk to me, Uncle. I need to hear your voice." Louis gazed upward and saw that his nephew was crying.

"I'm afraid to die, Uncle."

"There's nothing to be afraid of," Louis said. "You'll die quick and then to God you will go."

"What if you're wrong about Him? What if Jesus doesn't care about us?"

Louis sighed. "How can you say that after all you have seen? Look outside." Christopher went to the small window in the cage and peered downward.

"Do you see the flowers on that tree below? Do you see the sunflowers and the blooms? Every one of them is a gift from God to us."

"Aye, I do," Christopher answered.

"Do you see the sky? Do you see the clouds, the river, the grass, the sand, and even the birds?"

Suddenly, Christopher laughed. "There's a bird on that blooming tree. It's got small green wings and a red head. How did you know there was a bird?"

"Faith, I don't need to see outside to know that a bird would love the bugs those flowers bring."

Christopher nodded. "Then I shouldn't need to see Jesus to know that he loves me."

"For He gave His only beloved son so that we may have eternal life," Louis quoted the Bible. "Have faith, Nephew, it is the only thing we have left."

The door swung open and in came Bella. She no longer had chains around her. She ran to Louis and flung herself upon him in a loving embrace. Louis didn't look at her, he couldn't. Instead, he kept his eyes on the door and the man standing in the doorway, Sir Lawry.

"You're quite a man to give me your wife. I'd never seen that in all the years of my being a knight, nor have I ever seen a man beg forgiveness but not for his life, only to be forgiven."

"Take her from me," Prince Louis said, fighting every bone in his body not to kiss her cheeks, her mouth and her face.

Bella grasped his face and forced him to look into her sad eyes. "I love you, Louis! Why did you do that? I'd rather die than be without you."

Prince Louis couldn't answer. When he saw her like this, all he wanted to do was tell her how much he loved her, too, that every second he knew she was Sir Lawry's was enough to drive him mad.

"You are a selfless man, Louis," Sir Lawry said. "Do you know what my knights are saying? They are saying you are a better man than our king. That your heart is bigger, and your faith is stronger."

Louis took the block and with it, gently pushed Bella away.

"Leave me, woman! Go to your new husband. I want you no longer to love me."

"How can you say that?" Bella gasped. "Don't you know how I feel about Jacob Lawry?"

"That's exactly what I mean!" Louis roared. "Leave me! I saw how you feel about that man; it kills me! Go to him and feel for me no more after I am dead!"

Bella screamed. It wasn't a scream of terror or anxiety, but one of frustration and hopelessness. She rushed from him and pushed Sir Lawry out of her way to leave.

"I know what my knights see, but I see something else."

"What is that?" Louis rolled his eyes.

"A man I admire."

Shocked by that, Louis stood. "I see a man who my wife loves, though she denies it. I gave you my most valuable treasure, take her and be gone. Why must you come and throw it in my face that she is now yours? Haven't you heard that I shall die tomorrow? I shall die because I was once a very bad man, a man who does not deserve any admiration."

"Tomorrow, you become a martyr. I can see it now, the way my knights keep talking about you, about that cloth."

"Save your pity. I do not want it," Louis said.

"You won't find pity in me." Sir Lawry smiled. "Although, I still admire your foolishness."

"So, you think me a fool?" Louis asked.

"That I do, you gave me your wife. Your wife does love me, yes, but because she is my third cousin not because she wishes to ever be in my bed."

Louis whirled around, the block making it difficult.

"Aw, you finally opened your eyes. I said I'd marry her, but only because I don't wish my cousin to sold off and tortured by one of your enemies." With that, Lawry reopened the door. "You are a fool, Louis, more than me. I only took a wife who will never love me as a husband. But you, you will die knowing you pushed Bella away when all she wanted was to be with you one last time."

CHAPTER 21

Throughout the night Louis leaned in his corner, staring at the roaches running across the floor. One had a black stripe down the middle, the largest, which visited him in the night. It crawled up his boot and went inside. He could feel it crawling over his foot.

Bella loved him. He had judged her terribly. Sir Lawry was just a relative, not her lover. Their affection wasn't what he had thought. She hadn't kissed his lips; he suddenly remembered their last encounter. She had kissed his cheek.

Why did he think otherwise?

Prince Louis heard Christopher groaning in the corner of his cell. He didn't know what to say to comfort him. He'd seen many men dangle for quite some time before they choked to death. The rope wasn't always tied tight enough.

"Uncle," Christopher wailed. "I don't want to die. Please do something."

What can I do? What can I do but let the roaches crawl over my body? He was a man breathing his last breaths waiting for the sun to rise. Banging noises started to be heard coming through the window.

Christopher rushed to the window and then collapsed.

Louis didn't need to be told what was happening below in the courtyard. The sun would be up soon enough, and the knights had started building the platform from which they would be hung.

The prince thought of his wife, then his sister Sharera, his brother Delaney, and then his mother.

They would miss him.

Light began to creep in through the window. Christopher's head was tucked into his arms as if trying not to see the sun rising.

The banging noises started growing louder. The pounding made Louis' ears crawl as if they were hammering right next to him. Louis felt movement inside his boot and out rushed the big roach with the long stripe down its back. It stopped for a moment, staring back at him with long antennae waving and then scurried away into a hole in the stone wall.

More noise outside the window indicated a crowd gathering below; Louis could hear many conversations.

"Uncle, please, tell me…did you ever care for me?"

Louis, surprised by that question, answered, "You are my sister's son. How could I not?"

"Was I a good son to her?"

"Aye, you were. My sister loved you. She cried for weeks after you left. We searched for months for you."

"I'd do anything to say I'm sorry," Christopher cried. "I wish I could see my mother again before I die."

Prince Louis heard the door open. In came two knights with Sir Lawry in the center. He was dressed in full armor as were the two men beside him. "Are you going to war?"

"The king has ordered us to attack Cambone after you both are dead. We are to bring your head and throw it at your sister and King Cambone's royal feet."

"I don't think my head will look as good severed from my body," Louis said. One of the knights laughed. Sir Lawry glared at him, and he quickly stopped.

"What's the matter, Cousin-in-law?"

Sir Lawry grabbed the board around Prince Louis' neck and pulled him to his feet. Louis wobbled for a moment and then Sir Lawry took the key and freed his wrists and head. Louis tried to move his hands but couldn't. They felt stiff and then the sensation of pins and needles ran down his arms painfully.

"Don't jest," Sir Lawry muttered, clasping Prince Louis' legs in irons and then his wrists. The irons barely made it around his swollen wrists. When they did, they locked together with a loud click.

The knight who had laughed went to Christopher's cell and unlocked it. Christopher shook with fear as the man began attaching chains to his wrists. "As King Lightenwood's First Knight, Sir Lawry, I must tell you that you have been ordered to be hanged by the executioner this day."

Louis smiled. "I'll die a happy man knowing you'll look after the woman I love."

"Have no fear," Sir Lawry again promised. "I shall. She'll never worry about food, clothing or clean water. But a broken heart, I can never mend."

Prince Louis moved to Bella's cousin with the chains dragging between his legs. "Walk with me, Sir Lawry."

"Pardon, Uncle, but I feel no need to rush to death." Christopher wiped his eyes.

"Have faith." Louis smiled.

Christopher raised a brow and then walked beside his Uncle through the dungeon. Down the stairs, they made their way slowly to the wooden doors. Outside were all of the king's men in armor and on top of horses. Killing the two of them was only a pastime until they could get to the real murdering in Cambone, Louis realized.

Underneath the blooming tree was a stand. Bella was there. She looked horrible. Her eyes were swollen as if she hadn't slept. Louis moved toward her, ignoring the stares of the knights. His nephew did his best to keep up.

"Uncle, why hurry to die!"

Louis glanced back to his nephew.

"You will not die this day."

CHAPTER 22

Louis dragged his chains and stood beside his wife on the platform. Bella couldn't look at him. She lowered her head and grasped the fingers of his hands.

"I love you," he said.

"I can't do this. I won't," she said.

"Bella!" the king's familiar voice roared over the sound of the crowd. Louis slowly pivoted and saw that the king was atop a white stallion, wearing a royal blue coat with the emblem of a two-headed snake. The king was the only one that wasn't dressed for war, but instead wore fine clothes as if to go to a celebration.

"Put the noose around Louis Vincent's and Christopher's neck and be quick about it!"

She started to weep. "I won't kill him! I won't!"

Before the king could threaten her, Louis said, "I have one more request, My King."

"I allowed you to speak during your sentencing. You have no Royal rights now."

Louis stepped forward to the end of the platform. "I shall give you the whereabouts of King Vincent, my father's tomb. Inside are treasures so grand that your children's children could build dozens of kingdoms in your honor."

King Lightenwood dismounted. "The tomb, you'll tell me where your father's tomb is? I heard of it having living gold!"

Louis remembered the goldfish swimming in the tomb's underground pond. "I assure you the legends are true."

Without a second of thought, King Lightenwood blurted out: "Tell me! Tell me where your father's treasures are kept!"

"Let me live as well as my nephew. Free my wife of obligation of murder. Let us go."

King Lightenwood's smile dropped; his face curled into a frown. "Never, I'd rather die a pauper than let my father's killer live." He turned to Bella. "Do as I say, woman! Hang them! Put the rope around their necks and pull the latch!"

"My nephew knows the location of my father's tomb. He went there as a boy and saw my father buried. Christopher can tell you himself, if you let him live."

King Lightenwood bit his lower lip. He thought for quite some time. "All right, Christopher shall live a ten-year sentence in prison before being released."

Glancing over his left shoulder, he saw Christopher's head nodding yes.

Louis said to him, "Farewell, Nephew, remember me."

"I shall, Uncle. I'll never forget you saved my life," Christopher said, as several knights rushed towards him and began pulling him off of the platform.

King Lightenwood glared at Bella. "Now put the rope around his neck, Woman! Be done with it!"

Louis backed up to stand underneath the rope. He could see that the latch next to Bella would cause a trap door to drop below his feet. Soon, he would hang before her.

Her hands trembled above him as she reached to the rope and slowly pulled the noose down.

"Make it tight," Louis told her. "Or it won't be quick."

Bella pushed the rope away from his neck and held him. Their eyes met. He leaned down and kissed her lips stained with her tears. Prince Louis knew this would be the last time to taste her.

"You, Stable Boy, where is the dead man's linen you promised me?" Louis heard the king ask.

Prince Louis didn't move from the kiss to see if the linen was coming. All he wanted was this kiss to last forever. Heaven without her; it didn't seem worth going.

"It's here, my King," Mick said, bringing the shroud in a pouch to the platform.

The burial cloth of Jesus was laid across a high tree branch and it dangled next to them. Bella must have heard it whipping in the breeze.

Bella pulled away. "No, not this way."

King Lightenwood stepped onto the platform. He grabbed Bella's arm. "Take the latch!"

"I love you," she said to her prince.

"I'll love you forever and a day."

"I love you, too, forever and a day." Louis fought back his tears.

The king shoved her to stand next to the lever that pulled the trap door. He took the noose and wrapped it around Louis' neck loosely. "I've had enough of you and this cloth," he mumbled.

"Look at Louis Vincent the Be header," a knight below cried out.

"He cries like a baby over a woman."

"Silence!" roared the king; he reached out his hand and a knight came through the men and handed the king a torch.

"Watch it burn." The king moved the torch to the bottom of the burial shroud.

Louis yelled loud enough so all could hear. "This cloth has been spared from many fire!"

King Lightenwood backhanded Prince Louis with his chainmail-clad hand. "Your God shall die with you." He walked over to the shroud and raised the flame to the bottom where the imprint of the feet of Jesus lay crossed over one another.

"Pull the latch, Woman!" King Lightenwood yelled at her. "Either you do it or I will drop this torch where you stand, and you shall burn with your husband for all of eternity!"

A bright light began to form at where the fire was touching the shroud. Glowing, the light suddenly began to take a shape of a man, a man with the wings of a bird. Flames from the torch rolled off of him as he stood in front of the shroud, protecting it.

Knights began to scream and fall back. The women cried out in horror. King Lightenwood backed down the steps, dropping the torch to the ground.

From the mouth of the winged man came a wind which extinguished the flame at the imprint of Jesus' feet on the shroud. Suddenly his wings opened, and a sound came from its lips. It was almost a song.

"Jesus died for each and every one of you. Drop your swords and live in peace." The creature then opened his wings so far Louis could no longer see the people through the light.

Louis squinted and asked, "Brodan?" He thought he knew the voice. "Is that you?" Suddenly, Brodan's face appeared before him.

"Teach them."

Then, as quickly as the angel appeared, the creature flew upwards into the brilliant morning sky. Bella ran to Louis and pulled the rope from around his neck. She then grabbed the shroud and yanked it down from the tree.

"Kill them all!" screamed King Lightenwood, drawing his sword.

Thunder crashed overhead. The king looked up, but the noise wasn't coming from the heavens. Louis realized it was coming from over the hill. Thousands of Crusaders were coming, heading straight for the castle. The sign of the cross was on white pennons flying in the breeze.

The Crusaders from Cambone! Louis recognized the flags from his sister's kingdom.

"Line up!" King Lightenwood yelled. "Get ready to fight!"

CHAPTER 23

Louis and Bella rushed down from the platform. Bella began stuffing the shroud back into the pouch the stable hand had left. When the pouch was full, she turned to Prince Louis and said, "Finally, it is safe again."

Prince Louis' mind was on other things than the shroud. Louis locked eyes with several knights who were looking at the hundreds of Christian Crusaders coming on horseback. The knights glanced at him and then back at King Lightenwood, as if trying to decide what to do.

King Lightenwood is no longer in control of these knights. The knights weren't lining up, nor were they coming forward to cause the Crusaders or Bella any harm. No, they had just seen an angel, something magnanimous, a miracle.

Louis grabbed his wife's hand and pulled her in the direction of the Crusaders, away from Lightenwood's men.

"After them!" King Lightenwood commanded.

"I ordered you to fight!"

The king yanked a knight off his horse and mounted his steed. He drew his sword and started after Louis and Bella. Louis whirled Bella around to stand behind him. The sword was held up, ready to strike. Suddenly, Sir Lawry rammed Lightenwood's horse with his own mare.

Lightenwood's horse rose on its hind legs to avoid further collision with the other horse. The king tumbled to the ground with a thud.

"Take my horse, Prince." Sir Henry came forward and handed Prince Louis the reins of his steed. "Go to the Crusaders and tell them there will be no war this day."

When Louis saw the mighty mare, he recalled Sir Henry said it to be the fastest. Perhaps when Lightenwood's men come out of their shock, they wouldn't be able to catch them. Prince Louis mounted quickly and pulled Bella to sit in front of him on the horse.

His nephew! Where was he?

"Chris!" Louis called out.

Christopher ran out from the knights. Sir Lawry dismounted and gave the young man his seat.

The front rider of the Crusaders was wearing the cross on the front of his chest. As Prince Louis, Bella and Christopher drew closer, Louis discovered that the man leading the Crusaders was none other than his brother, King Delaney of Valtearea. Next to his brother was his sister Queen Sharera and King Darren of Cambone. He knew Sharera was tough as nails, but to ride with the Crusaders, how improper of a Queen!

Prince Louis, Princess Bella and Prince Christopher were soon in front of their royal family. King Delaney raised his hand and the Crusaders stopped. Prince Christopher dismounted when he saw Sharera, his mother. Queen Sharera jumped off her horse and hugged him.

"Son!" she cried out.

"Christopher, take your mother back to Cambone castle at once," Louis ordered.

"We fight for the shroud," Queen Sharera said.

"Bella has it." Prince Louis held up the bag. "Bella will go with you." The Crusaders began to ready themselves for a battle. Prince Louis waited until Bella was off the stallion, grabbed Sharera's sword and then went to the front.

"Lightenwood's men claim they no longer want war this day!"

The Jacksvilla knights started coming slowly on horseback. Sir Lawry was leading them. Suddenly, Sir Lawry raised a hand. The knights stopped; both sides stared at one another.

"Toss down your swords, Crusaders from Cambone," Sir Lawry yelled.

The Crusaders would never surrender, Louis knew. "We think not. You toss down yours." Sir Lawry nodded and King Lightenwood's knights, hundreds of them, began tossing their weapons onto the ground below.

"What?" Prince Louis gasped.

Next, Lightenwood's knights began to toss down their helmets, too, and dripped off the snake emblems from their garments.

"What is this?" Prince Louis asked Sir Lawry.

Sir Lawry jumped off a horse and went to stand before Prince Louis and King Delaney with lowered head. "We've come to join you, not fight against you."

Prince Louis smiled.

"And Lightenwood?" Louis glanced back at the king standing next to the platform alone. He wondered what would happen to him.

"What of your king?"

"He's not much of a king without an army." Sir Lawry returned the smile. Prince Louis made sure his wife and the shroud were secure, and then he glanced to Sir Lawry.

"Why do you want to join us?"

"We want to protect the shroud with you. Can we serve you?" Sir Lawry asked both kings.

The King of Valtearea and the King of Cambone nodded yes in unison. "So be it." Sir Lawry took a Crusader flag from one of Cambone's men.

"Then let's go back to Valtearea and rebuild Valtearea castle. We need a place to protect the shroud. It is a reminder of what Jesus Christ did for us." Louis heard weeping. His sister, Queen Sharera was still hugging her long lost son. The smile on his brother and brother-in-law's faces, said it all, war between the lands was finally over. King Lightenwood was powerless.

Peace now reigned among the nations.

Prince Louis snapped the horse's reins and trotted through the enormous group of Crusader knights with his Royal family and his new friends. Together, they gathered into one massive army.

His wife, Princess Bella, glanced back at him with those beautiful eyes and kept smiling with her red, luscious lips.

Oh, he would have her again, as his wife. For forever and eternity.

Their new future was as bright as the sun.

ABOUT THE AUTHOR

Michele Wallace Campanelli is an American writer, singer and celebrity. During the early 1990s, Michele was lead singer of the heavy metal band, Black Widow, which was one of the first all-female bands in Florida during the early 90s. After the band, Michele Wallace Campanelli started writing short stories and fiction novels professionally. She has had nine stories appearing on the best-sellers list, including two that reached #1 on the New York Times. Her short stories have been included in over 30 international selling anthologies. She has also penned numerous novels, magazine and newspaper articles in both fiction and non-fiction published by Simon & Schuster, Chronicle Books, Fireside Books, Fiction wise, Florida Today Newspaper, Woman's World Magazine, Adamsmedia, McGraw-Hill, Multnomah Books, Red Rock Press, HCI and America House Publishing. Over 57 million people have read her written works internationally. In 1998, Michele wed Louis V. Campanelli III at St. Mark's UMC in Indialantic, Florida. In June 2012 Louis passed away. She currently lives in Brevard. When Michele isn't writing, she is CEO of Regal Entertainment Services LLC which performs concerts around Florida. She is a professional singer, writer and actor. As a devoted Christian, she uses her talents to glorify God and bring joy to others through music and her books.